DRAWING THE LINE

No Ladies in Room A3

CLARE SCOPES

About the Author

Clare lives in Melbourne, Australia with her four-legged companion and a semi-petrified spider by the name of George. She has a Bachelor of Arts in Cinema, Womens Studies and Spanish and studied Professional Writing and Editing at RMIT University. After many attempts to write a novel Clare has finally triumphed with *Drawing The Line*, a work of historical fiction with significant romantic leanings.

Acknowledgments

Thanks to all my excellent friends, family and neighbours for their love, support and advice. A special thanks to my beta readers and proofers, Eve, Dorothy, Helena, Ian, Jocelyn, Rachel and Sabine. Thanks to Lorraine and Cheryl for their deposits of schnitzels and cakes, and to Chris for putting the bins out.

$\mathcal{M}$aggie Goodwin eyed the slightly terrifying man on the other side of the desk and let out a long breath. The big cheese of Harley Studios was less imposing than she'd expected—his reputation having projected a man of greater stature in her mind's eye. But he *was* sitting down so perhaps his legs were longer than his compact torso suggested.

"If you just give me a half a chance Mr Harley I promise to make myself useful. *Very* useful. Matter of fact I plan on being a great animator—"

"Animator?" He plugged the stick of tobacco in his mouth and snapped open a gold lighter.

"Yes like you—well not *exactly* like you. But a great animator all the same." Maggie paused, allowing a suitable interval for the tapping of cigarette on desk, "I've followed your career with a great deal of interest, a great deal."

"Not too great I hope." He snorted, coughed into his fist and let out a weary sigh, "let's take a look then."

The folio slid across the desk and he slapped it open, examining the pages with little apparent interest before singling out a conventional seascape, the result of a lazy afternoon spent with paints at Coney Island. "Watercolor?"

"That's right." Maggie's dark head bent closer as his finger passed over the stiff paper.

"Got any more of them?"

"Not here…you see I thought, well I thought you'd like to meet my squirrel." Without further ado she took control of the situation and flipped back to the front pages, "here…my squirrel —gets herself into all sorts of trouble, an adventurer like Wild Willie…"

Her smile faded, her heart thumping and hands folded in her lap contritely. His reaction wasn't quite the one she'd hoped for. In fact it bore little resemblance to the one entertained on the long trip across the country from New York to California. "Of course she needs a name, something like Suzie or Sally or Shirley perhaps—no not Shirley—squirrel's not one for dancing on tables in silly dresses—"

"So you're one of those women huh?" Milton Harley said, flipping through the remaining sketches with rough impatience. He ground out his cigarette and frowned pointedly at his pant-wearing applicant, "you prefer pants to silly dresses?"

"Oh they're just the thing for long hours at a desk, terribly comfortable. What's good for the goose is good for the gander wouldn't you say? I believe in progress, new ways and all that— are you a Utopian? *The Los Angeles Times* seems to think so."

"I don't believe in groups." He shot her a stern look and returned to the dull seascape assigned by her equally dull art teacher.

"I just know *The Little Orphan* will be a terrific success—it's positively marvelous what you've done here, built this…this great incubator of talent."

"Incubator eh? You get that from some magazine?"

"Perhaps…yes I suppose I may have…" Maggie colored and they exchanged a small smile, "but the point is Mr Harley, I've come all the way across the country to incubate, work my way up and learn from the best. The best of the best."

"Miss Goodwin. Let me set you straight. We don't employ lady animators."

"But why ever not?"

"You know very well why not."

"Well…no, I'm afraid I don't Mr Harley…sir."

He shook his head, clearly irritated, "because there *are* no lady animators…it's as simple as that."

Maggie swallowed and lowered her eyes. His logic was clearly faulty but it wouldn't do to push. Not now, at least. His cigarette glowed orange and he drew back hungrily, his eyes closed and brow furrowed. "You're no doubt aware the position is in the Paint and Ink Room with the rest of my girls…and very fine girls they are too."

"Well all the same I'd like to dip my toe in with my squirrel," Maggie said, gracing him with a generous smile she hoped might go a ways to soften his resolve.

"Dip your toe in?"

"Get it wet, metaphorically," Maggie pressed on, unable to stop now her toe was fully-dipped, "dive in the deep-end. Yes— that's precisely what I meant in the first place, not the toe at all—"

"Miss Goodwin. Will you kindly quit your yammering." He combed his fingers through silvering hair then let out a curmud- geonly grunt, gray-blue eyes resting just shy of her chin, "you're not afraid of hard work? Am I right on that account?"

"Not a bit. You can count on it. I won't let you down."

"And you're not married?"

"No, not married."

"Guess you'll get round to it," he decided, "when you come across the right fella…Now listen up. I won't tolerate lateness, laziness or any other kind of slacking off, that understood?"

"Yes Mr Harley, no slacking off. Got it."

"One week's training then it's the real thing—if you make the cut."

"I'm hired?" Maggie's heart pounded, and as she extended her long arm across the table to shake on the deal the boss of Harley Studios winked, a steady stream of smoke issuing from his nose.

"Welcome to the family. You'll do very nicely down at Paint and Ink, very nicely indeed."

Maggie marched from Building D, her face flushed with joy and mind racing to distant lights. She would start at the bottom and work her way up, prove she was no bad bet despite being a member of the fairer sex. She whistled softly, following yet another pretty path edged with shrubs in bloom.

"Hallo, sun." She smiled up at the perfect accompaniment to her growing fortune, the great yellow engine in the wide, blue sky, and as she left the lot she gazed back at her new home. *She* was part of the family now, the great Milton Harley had said so himself. "Heck—sorry old girl, I forgot all about you." She turned on her heel and ran back in, holding onto her hat for good measure. It was, as usual, too loose and in danger of taking flight and nesting in the nearest tree, or getting squashed under the wheels of a careless bus.

She rounded the hood of the ancient jalopy that had kindly but jerkily transported her from Huntington Park to Burbank. It would take some doing, getting used to her new identity as automobile owner. "I did it," she whispered as the rusty ignition turned.

But there was no familiar spluttering and coughing, no engine rumbling violently to life, no plume of smoke spewing from the blackened thingamajig at the back. She squinted at the instruments and patted the steering-wheel encouragingly, "come along Bertha—"

"Don't press the pedal so much," came a man's voice from out of the blue. Maggie, her face a perfect picture of consternation, turned to the tall rather gangly man standing by the passenger door.

"But I thought the pedal was supposed to make her go?"

"It does, but she's flooded, sounds like."

"Flooded?" Maggie drew her chin to her neck, incredulous at the thought, "seems unlikely in a desert, but I'll take your word for it."

"May I?" he asked, but before she had time to answer, he'd already wrestled the hood open and begun an investigation.

"Any luck down there?" Maggie hollered a few moments later, her head poking from the window in an effort to hear the diagnosis, "you see I need Bertha to keep me out of trouble. Mr Harley won't tolerate lateness and I'm determined not to disappoint—nothing worse than disappointing, don't you agree? Hallo...?" Maggie stepped out of the car and stood close to the kind stranger tinkering with Bertha's innards, "so that's her heart is it?"

"Ow!" he cried out, his forehead colliding with the hood's sharp edge.

"Good heavens! Are you hurt? Take off your hat and let's see where she bit you—"

"No no, no damage done," he pulled the brim down and returned to the business at hand, scowling, his teeth gritted in pain, "afraid I can't say the same for this old thing."

"Poor Bertha. Poor _you_." She held out her hand, "Maggie—how do you do?"

"Why I..." He frowned at his grease-stained hands, and as a flush rose from the collar of his shirt, he tipped his hat in greeting. "Ted."

"Pleased to meet you Ted."

"Likewise."

"So what's the prognosis doc?" She affected a look of grave concern, "will the old girl survive?" He eyed the hood warily and lowered it onto the latch.

"Prognosis? You oughta get her to the shop before she croaks, way I see it."

"Heck." Maggie's humor, generally maintaining the flow of a jaunty stream, suddenly drained away like water down a manhole. "I didn't expect—why it's a disgrace…back to the shop? We only just left, right Bertha?" She patted her metal friend then smiled at her companion, "you'll have to excuse my strange affection for a machine but she's the only friend I've got in Los Angeles, well apart from the sun that is."

"Sure," he nodded solemnly, wiped his fingers on a handkerchief extracted from his pocket and rested his hand on his hip, "lemmie guess, Sherman Auto, right?"

"Uh huh, right on Loyola Street."

"Biggest crooks in the business," he ran his hand over the badly-faded paintwork, "hop in and give her another whirl."

This time Bertha came to life with a great coughing and billowing of smoke. The motor chugged and rattled, shaking like an earthquake taking hold of the ground beneath them. Or perhaps it was an earthquake, Maggie mused. She'd been half-expecting one since arriving in the fault-lined state, not a big one, just a small one for starters to get the hang of it first. "That-a girl!" Maggie shouted above the valiant engine. But her jubilation was short-lived. After two more lurching chugs, Bertha once again fell silent.

"Must be on strike," Maggie deduced, screwing up her nose, "keeping up with the times are you old girl?" She turned to Ted, "why, a girl has to keep up with the fashion you understand—pants, strikes, don't you know?"

"Uh-huh." He pushed up his brim to get a better view of the talkative woman with the dancing face, "afraid the boss won't agree with you on that account." He stuffed the handkerchief back in his pocket and escorted her from the vehicle.

"No," Maggie agreed as she made a quick appraisal of the man with a knack for machines. Tall, fair-skinned and with something familiar about his well put-together face, "although I don't suppose anyone would think to strike here—Mr Harley is terrific, just terrific. Not exactly sold on my squirrel but he was rather taken with Coney Island. Are you part of the Harley family too?"

"You could say that."

"An animator?"

"Nope," he shook his head emphatically, "not if my life depended on it."

"Why I don't suppose it'll come to that." She let out a rich laugh and he grinned, "do you know Art Schrieber by any chance? Well of course you must do—everyone knows Art Schrieber…"

"Sure, we're acquainted."

"He's the bee's knees and all that…well, *evidently.*" She turned away, coloring slightly—she hadn't meant to gush, regurgitate silly phrases from magazine gossips.

"I'll take your word for it." His hands dug in his pockets, coins jingling as he stared at the ground.

"A great artist," she said in a more suitable tone.

"Well he sure made us a ton of money, gotta give him that."

"Oh," Maggie frowned, "but money isn't the only measure of success is it? At least I hope it isn't."

"Can't do much without the stuff." He plunged his hands deeper and the jingling intensified, "hang tight and I'll call my man down at Bingleys, get you a tow."

As Ted made off towards the maze of Harley buildings, striding away to whatever job it was his job to do, Maggie's mind got to work. He seemed like a nice enough fellow—and certainly nice enough to see to an introduction between her good self and the reportedly witty and rather handsome Art Schrieber.

The city passed by as she trundled along Jefferson Boulevard. "The City of Angels," Maggie whispered, feasting her eyes on stout buildings with sensuous curves…so unlike the Manhattan towers reaching skywards like overcrowded seedlings jostling for light. Another block went by and another scene came into view, a line of men in worn-out clothes queuing for goods, perhaps flour or sugar or canned meats. She'd seen half-a-dozen similar types taking too-long a rest in the train station the day she'd arrived, the attendant shooing the desperate men away like rats.

Nevertheless, Maggie reminded herself, the country was back on its feet thanks to Roosevelt and the WPA. Dignity had taken a hit, but men, women and children had not starved, or so her father said.

At Florence Avenue she stepped off the steel-wheeled machine and stowed her map in her pocket. Apart from a brief wave of claustrophobia and a poke in the temple with a wayward elbow, the trip on the trolley-car hadn't been so bad.

All was well. Marvelous, in fact. She had a job, a new home, and the man from Bingleys— arriving soon after Ted's departure —had identified the problem within a shake of a leg. The new thingamajig would cost eight dollars fifty to be fitted, after the old one was taken out she supposed. Not a great sum, but enough to exceed her weekly budget, an austere figure plucked from nowhere in her determination to get along without the securities of home.

After a short walk Maggie arrived at her apartment. The gate swung open and she raced upstairs, calling down to her neighbor below. "That's a spiky-looking devil isn't it?" The man nodded curtly then returned to tending one of the many potted cacti invading the sunny courtyard. She very much planned on taking a closer look, getting out her pencils and making a proper study of their fat needle-pocked bodies, some of them sprouting rather surprising pink, white or yellow flowers.

Before passing through Arizona she'd only ever seen such plants in cartoons, or in books in the library, the quiet too-chilly room her father barely set foot in due to his trips to Washington to be of help to the government. The exact details of William Goodwin's job remained a mystery to his one and only child, but it was safe to say he was a man of great reputation and much admired by Roosevelt himself.

Her new home, apartment six with the burnt-orange door and dangerously loose handle had a very particular odor. Not exactly musky, and certainly not damp, but very particular nevertheless. After discarding her shoes—tossed into the nearest corner, she passed under the archway into the living-room. A solitary sofa-chair sat to the left of the window to catch the best light, and next to it a dear little table she'd swapped for a dime at the junk store not two blocks away. Once she'd added her own personal touches, some knickknacks and pretty furnishings to cheer the place up, it would be homely enough.

"My blue-sky life," she said, heaving the stubborn window open and surveying the street below. A decent enough neighborhood, or at least not dangerous, she figured. The few shady characters who'd called out from across the street yesterday were simply men with bad manners who ought to know better.

Her stomach grumbled in protest, quite aware of the barren state of the kitchen cupboards…one pack of soda crackers, one can of baked beans, some coffee, and a rather solid-sounding hunk of bread. She stared at the sink, scoffing the crackers and contemplating her new state of independence…attending to basics had always been someone else's business at the Goodwin household.

She would have to learn to cook. Or take a trip to PJ's for another forty-cent hamburger. She plucked the last cracker from the pack and nodded to herself, deciding to do just that—remove the awful flaccid pickle and add more sauce.

Chapter Two

The next morning she showered briskly, dressing as usual in one of her four pairs of tailored pants, her neatest pair of sneaks and a short-sleeved blouse. She wasn't sure if Milton disapproved of her skirt-shirking per se, but his flagging of her pants had been duly noted. She grinned, yanking the door open with fresh gusto. The boss of Harley Studios and creator of Wild Willie thought her out of the ordinary, and that was exactly what she wanted.

"How should I know?" said the woman next to Maggie, one among the small group of trainees gathered outside Room 27, Building C.

"Sure he will," said another. She made a dreamy face and sighed.

"Geez—she's dizzy on the guy already," the first said, rolling her eyes theatrically.

"I'll have you know we get along just *fine*." After a brief silence, the two women looked at each other and burst into gay laughter. "Shush! It's him—"

As Milton Harley approached the group of new recruits Maggie considered his considerable reputation. According to reports, confirmed and unconfirmed, the founder and boss of Harley Studios was not only the 'bee's knees' but 'plenty rugged' *and* blessed with an authority that 'fit like a well-worn suit'. As such, in the process of going about his manly business of etching a great and indelible mark upon the world at large, he'd left a string of broken hearts behind him, not to mention a failed marriage and three broken engagements.

"How do you do, ladies?" He swiped his nose, fiddled with an unlit cigarette and gestured to the woman at his side, a stern type of around forty with large unblinking eyes and a neat component of hair, "this is Miss Donnelly. Mary won't stand for any messing about, understand?" He lit the cigarette and narrowed his eyes, "you got two weeks to prove yourself ladies, so let's see what you're made of."

"Yes sir Mr Harley," said the woman in grave danger of losing her heart. Her blushing smile was rewarded with a wink.

"That's the ticket. Mary'll get you started, run you through the rules then its up to you. We got a whole bunch of work to do so get to it like your life depended on it." He winked again, "got that?"

"We'll get that Little Orphan in the can," Maggie rallied from the back of the pack.

Before falling asleep with a dry mouth and a stomach full of hamburger, Maggie had taken it upon herself to bone up on all things Harley. If there were no more delays *The Little Orphan* was on track to make capital-H-history as the world's first feature-length color animation—unless Independent Studios pulled a rabbit out of the hat and beat them to it. "We won't let Independent beat us," Maggie enthused, her comment seemingly falling on deaf ears.

"I'll let you get to it." Milton's smile waned and a look of consternation took its place. He turned on his heel, and without another word, headed in the direction of more urgent business.

"Ready?" Mary glanced over her shoulder as she led the way into Paint and Ink. Maggie's eyes bugged. Her new home, Room 27C was not only astonishingly vast but entirely filled with rows of silent women painting on celluloid sheets. "How's the forest coming along, Harriet?" Mary asked as they stopped by one of the desks.

"Oh you know, so so." Harriet looked up, her face tight. She stretched her arms over her head then hid a yawn behind a gloved hand.

"Come along," Mary said to the group, seemingly annoyed.

"Is that her? The Orphan?" Maggie enquired, lingering behind to watch a perfect inky line trail from the tip of Harriet's paintbrush.

"That's right." The line continued on its way, rounding the curve of the Orphan's back and into the hollow of her impossibly narrow waist.

"Beautiful," Maggie muttered, awed by the painstaking precision of the mark, "so long," she said, rushing off to catch up with the tour.

"Twenty-four cells for every second of film," Mary explained as they passed between rows of desks, "hurry along, we can't waste a second." She reached the end of the hive-like room and turned to face her students, "this is where you'll find your paint."

Maggie whistled softly. The entire back wall was entirely devoted to supplies, every shelf, cupboard and drawer filled with pots of paint in every size and color, each with its proper place—a system not to be violated on any account. Girls getting lazy with lids would be punished harshly, and it went without saying— respect for tools was a habit to adopt from day one.

"Each character has their own color chart, it's all set out in the manuals. Take 214 C for instance," Mary said, shooting Maggie a pointed look as she removed a pot from the meticulously labelled shelf, "look familiar? Well it ought to. This pink is our good friend Willie's ears—the inner part to be precise."

Maggie's senses sharpened. At last the lecture had begun to get interesting now Mary was done with rules and regulations. But the scolding soon returned. The Paint and Ink Room was to be run like clockwork. Strict rules were just that, strict rules—to be followed at all costs. *Never* leave paintbrushes unwashed under any circumstances, *always* wear the white glove to prevent scratching or smudging, *defer* the urge to gossip until lunch which would take place at noon and last until one.

"I don't have to remind you girls—one hour is one hour," Mary said, plucking at her sleeve with great irritation. She wasn't to hear about headaches or stomach troubles or the trials and tribulations of the morning rush-hour, and if the traffic was really so bad that the red-car moved slower than a dopey snail, then a girl must rise earlier to take the situation into account.

She peered over her spectacles and issued her final edict for the running of a smooth shop. A girl was never to assume, "if any of you are ever unsure about anything—" and she meant anything, then a girl had only to ask. Maggie grinned as they pressed on. She would draw her squirrel with the very same expression that evening, bossing around a bunch of naughty squirrel children, perhaps.

"How do you do? I'm Maggie." She shook hands with the woman assigned as her guide, a gorgeous bottle-blonde with a skirt as tight as snake-skin.

"Clara. Pleased to meetcha. That's Harriet."

"Why yes, hallo again—how do you do." She sat between her new colleagues and got familiar with her work-space, the adjustable desk sloped to accommodate long hours of close work.

"Got any questions ask her," Clara said, thumbing at Harriet.

"But aren't you my guide?"

"Only kidding," Clara mugged, "go ahead and bust your guts,

ask me all the questions you got," she twitched her hair-thin brows suggestively, "that's right, I got *all* the juicy gossip."

"Well…I rather think we oughta save that for lunch," Maggie said primly, eager to get on with the job of proving herself.

"Sure," Clara snorted, "I got all the answers, but Harriet'll protect you from Sergeant Mary."

"Oh…how's the Orphan coming along?" Maggie turned to Harriet, who, unlike Clara, wasn't wearing a skirt strangling her thighs like a boa constrictor.

"Still lost in the forest," Harriet let out a sigh, "but the prince will come soon."

"Let me help speed things up then," Maggie said, surveying the battalion of women armed with paintbrushes, pots and thumbless gloves. She turned to Clara, "where do I start?"

Clara rested her brush in a dish, stood, and beckoned Maggie to follow. "Come on, come on," she flapped her hand impatiently and extracted a sheet of celluloid from a nearby drawer, "see, what ya do is grab one of these suckers, and one of these suckers…" After opening another draw marked with mysterious code she led Maggie to yet more storage compartments, "and when you're done with all the pretty colors you stick it in here—see?"

"Swell," Maggie said, uncertain and somewhat put off by Clara's lack of reverence for the craft, "thank you Clara."

"Oh yeah—plus you gotta make sure it's dry. Here, start you off with old Willie for practice. Till you get the swing of it."

As Maggie slipped on the glove and took up her brush she gaped at the outline of Wild Willie. After all, Art Schrieber had more than likely drawn the original himself.

"Start at the left," Harriet suggested as Maggie's brush hovered over the cell.

"That figures." Maggie pursed her lips, dipped the delicate brush and set about painting Willie's speed-flattened body with a familiar brown.

"Try and get it in one go," Harriet advised, demonstrating the technique.

"Ah-ha, got it…*much* better."

Exactly what mischief Wild Willie was up to, freed from the context of background and other players, Maggie could only guess…perhaps escaping a trap set by his nemesis Drabble Duck. Or was Willie doing the chasing himself, about to succeed in whatever audacious plan he'd set in motion…? But one thing was certain, there would come a day when *her* squirrel would burst into life with just as much speed and comic grace as Wild Willie himself.

The paintbrush approached a tight spot and she faltered. "Heck—" Maggie frowned at the brown blot on her glove, the paint pooling messily and overshooting the edge of Willie's bulbous boot. She looked up to see Clara smiling at her knowingly.

"Not so easy, huh?"

"No. Perhaps not."

The hours passed and Willie's boots improved in both shape and quality, but as for his trade-mark stubby starfish-hands, more practice was clearly in order. "Step by step," Maggie muttered to herself as she perfected Willie's eyeball with a deft flick of the wrist. She felt a heavy presence behind her.

"Light, but swift," Mary instructed her new recruit.

"I just figured out how to twist the brush at the end," she informed her instructor proudly, "seems to help tremendously— I'm used to pencils you see, drawing my squirrel, but I'll get the hang of paint."

"Keep up the good work. We'll start you on the Orphan tomorrow."

"Lining or coloring?" Maggie inquired hopefully. Lining was the next step up on the ladder, and the quicker she climbed it the better.

"Coloring, let's not get ahead of ourselves."

"Yes Miss Donnelly." Lining or not. Maggie was glad to be making an impression.

Lunch took place, as promised, at exactly noon. The cafeteria was cheery, light, and like every other edifice on the Harley lot, rather vast. On one side were views to the central courtyard, a large square presided over by a giant statue of Wild Willie, Harley Studio's most famous and lucrative critter.

"No…" Maggie's mouth watered at the delicious sight behind the glass counter, the hearty fare about to be gobbled up by Harley's hungry hoards, "is that hotpot?"

"Don't waste your time," Harriet warned, "it's slop."

"Says you," Clara said, clearly offended. Maggie eyeballed the array of foods on offer, rolls and cold-cuts, baloney and sausage, steaming potatoes, macaroni and cheese.

"It all looks delicious."

"Yeah?" Clara scoffed, "well he ain't gonna feed us dog-soup is he? Milt's got deep pockets ya know," she flicked her eyebrows and feigned innocence, "least what I heard anyways…"

"Milt? You mean Mr Harley?" Maggie turned to Harriet for clarification.

"Clara's moving up in the world." Harriet slid her tray over to make room for Maggie.

"Course I mean Mr Harley—*geez*." Clara shook her head and adjusted her assets in her slinky top, "see you dummies later."

Too much lipstick, Maggie thought as Clara joined friends at a table at the far end of the room. There was no getting away from the fact, the girl was chintzy, from her platinum waves right down to her click-clack heels…the kind of glamour that looked better from afar, Maggie decided. *She* wouldn't dream of torturing her own mop into a stiff unnatural state, not in a million years. Not that there was anything wrong with following Hollywood trends—

pants for example. But if you were going to do it, Maggie figured, you ought to do it right.

She and Harriet found a free table and plonked themselves down, ravenous after the morning's work, their trays heavy with loaded plates and sodas. "Do you live far?" Maggie enquired politely, her fork poised to attack and fearing she might drool at any minute.

"Bunker Hill, you know it?"

"A hill? Oh I do love a view don't you? New York is just about as hilly as a flapjack—" Maggie paused mid-sentence, her attention taken by two men at the adjacent table—and one of them taking the lion's share of it.

Her heart skipped a beat. There was no mistaking, it was him. The intense, intelligent expression, the slightly too-long hair slicked into a helmet of waves.

"Too risky," his companion was saying, "I'm behind the eight-ball already."

"And another thing, tell that blabbermouth to watch his mouth," Art Schrieber said, looking up to meet the gaze of the staring woman.

"Why hallo there—how do you do?" She chewed hastily then swallowed, determined to grab the opportunity of meeting the Harley hero, even if her face was a little too red for the occasion, her mouth a little too full.

"She one of yours?" Art's companion said to him, giving Maggie the once-over.

"Nope—who's your friend?" Art enquired of Harriet.

"I'm Maggie, Maggie Goodwin."

"Maggie, meet Art and Bert," Harriet said as she mopped sauce from her plate and devoured the last of her bread.

"It's an honor to meet you Mr Schrieber, you see I'm one of you too, an animator I mean—or will be when I'm done with Paint and Ink."

"Done with Paint and Ink huh?" Art raised his brows and grinned at Bert, "well how do you like that?"

"I've been slaving away over boots and fingers all morning."

"She's a babe-in-training," Harriet explained.

"I get it. Bright-eyed and bushy-tailed."

"Sergeant Mary's giving her the lowdown so she knows what rules to break."

"Oh good heavens no," Maggie cried, "I don't plan on breaking any rules…good lord no."

"Ah, so you're the hard-work-reaps-rewards type?" Art said.

"I'm determined to prove myself," Maggie nodded, her flushing now abated.

"That so?" Art said with a smirk, "looks to me you're in the wrong company then." He directed a meaningful look at Harriet, who, seemingly still hungry, pressed crumbs to her fingertips and licked them clean.

"Speak for yourself."

"My squirrel's got a mind to be famous, she's a Wild Willie in the making."

"You better believe it, this one's got talent," Harriet confirmed, having just been introduced to the whip-smart critter as they'd stood in line for hotpot.

"Mr Harley says ladies have a feeling for color but motion's my thing, running and jumping and goodness knows what else—but you see she needs a lot of doing and I wondered…I wondered if you might be kind enough to lend a hand, help out with a little advice?"

"Sure. Why not, I'd be delighted, but call me Art okay?"

"Sure. Art," she stared, her head whirling at the prospect of getting more acquainted with the wavy-haired animator, "when can we—" she broke off, disappointed to see Art had already returned to his conversation with Bert. Their little tete-a-tete, it seemed, had come to a rather abrupt end.

"Mary's on the prowl," Clara said, arriving at their table. She narrowed her eyes at Harriet and drummed her fingers at her hip. Maggie, alarmed, jumped to her feet and turned to Harriet.

"Coming?"

"With you in a jiffy," she said, shooing her away, "go on, run along, don't worry bout me."

"Oh sure," Clara said, glaring over her shoulder as she and Maggie left, "I ain't worried one bit."

$\mathcal{M}$aggie jammed down her hat as Bertha bounced over potholes. She would need a tighter fit to combat the wind on the now-familiar drive to Harley Studios, but her identity had solidified. She was now Maggie Goodwin, animator in waiting and driver of automobile.

Three weeks had gone by in a flash. As promised, Bertha had been fitted with a new thingamajig and the old girl's engine could now be relied upon to splutter to life without nearly so much coughing as before. There'd be no more slow-poke trips on the red-car or risking the wrath of Sergeant Mary, and the man at Bingleys garage had refused to accept the tip offered in recompense for an earlier than usual start, the personal delivery of the jalopy right to Maggie's door.

The only real disappointment had been not crossing paths with Art again, by chance or intent. Not a single sighting since synchronicity had planted them on adjacent tables at the cafeteria on day one of her employment. The next time fate intervened she wouldn't let Mr Schrieber scurry off like one of his mischievous critters. At least not before they'd set a date to talk shop. Perhaps he might take her somewhere fancy for dinner, and, she figured, if he'd been skipping lunch for three whole weeks he would need a good feed.

Their chance encounter had left a lasting impression. She'd met important people before, government-men with the authority to change the law of the land, but Art's power was something altogether different. *Invigorating,* she decided as she drove through the studio-gates and squeezed Bertha's bulk between two rust-free much flashier cars. "Well done old girl." She wrenched the brake on, adjusted her hat and headed off to Paint and Ink.

By now Maggie's brush glided over celluloid with far more skill but significantly less gusto. In fact she'd begun to curse the Orphan's propensity to spin her voluminous skirt quite so often. The problem was, every day brought the same old thing. Blue. Blue. And still more blue.

However, she reminded herself, there *was* satisfaction to be had, a meditation of a kind, the sweeping of hand and wrist, just the right amount of paint on brush, a precision of judgement— enough to rouse one's pride and get through the long day. And she was certain her improvements had been noted, that Mary would soon sneak up behind her and announce her promotion, from painter of spaces to painter of lines.

The door of Room 27C opened with a gargantuan squeak and Maggie woke from her reverie. "Good morning girls," Milton boomed as Mary rose from her seat.

"Good morning Mr Harley," came the chorus of feminine voices. Maggie's gaze slid to Milt's companion with some surprise. Tall with broad shoulders, his body bent in a slight stoop. Ted. But without a hat. And not just without a hat but without hair as well. Indeed, his well-formed dome was as bald as an egg—but quite a lovely egg all the same, Maggie decided as she searched for signs of damage from Bertha's ungrateful attack. Thankfully, there were no apparent dents, dints or scratches, at least none detectable from a distance of thirty feet.

"What's he doing here?" Harriet hissed.

"Beats me." Clara crossed her legs and bounced her foot in an eye-catching manner, "hallo there boss…" She made her eyes wide, thrust out her chest and he suppressed a pleased grin.

"Good morning, ah, Clara. Good morning girls. Listen up, I got important news…"

"Look out—" Harriet shot Maggie an urgent look.

"We're all required to make sacrifices from time to time, yes?" Milton paused as he rose on his toes and rocked back to his heels, his gaze moving from one end of the room to the other, his regard both fond and paternal, "and this particular occasion will require *great* sacrifice, I think you'll agree…"

"Sure thing boss." Clara saluted and shot him an impish grin as Ted, tool-box in hand, squinted and scanned the room.

"So that being said I'd like your time on Saturday," the boss went on.

"Saturday?" Harriet muttered, "gimmie a bonus and I'll think it over—"

"No ifs or buts, understand? I expect every one of you to make an effort. We're all in this together, right ladies?" Milton smiled and waved a nicotine-stained finger, his eyes sparkling behind billowing smoke, "Saturday *night*, that is—"

The room erupted with cries of delight then subsided to excited chatter. "So with that being said I'll see you at the Palomar, dressed to the nines no *later* than nine…and that's an order you hear?"

"The Palomar!" Clara shouted, clapping her hands madly.

"Palomar?" Maggie turned to Harriet for help.

"The dancehall you ninny—and boy is it fancy!"

Despite Clara's disdain being as plain as the clearest of clear days, it was, Maggie noted with some wonder, not plain enough to ruin the effect of her delectable face. "A little thank you for all your hard work now our Orphan's on the home-straight," Milton said, his brow furrowing as he coughed, a rich rattle emanating from deep in his chest, "or thereabouts, ballpark figure…usually is with these things, so let's knuckle-down and make a dash to the finish-line eh? Hit a home run."

"Yes sir Mr Harley but I got a condition okay?" Clara said, giving a fair impression of May West, "you only dance with *me*…"

"Now that wouldn't be fair on the other girls now would it?" He cleared his throat, tugged his sleeve and winked, "show me you deserve it and we'll see."

"I know, I know—*whats you put in is whats you get out*," Clara pouted as Milton turned to Mary.

"Ed's here for the drawer. Which one's bust?" And without further ado, the boss left them to it.

"Let's see," Mary led Ted to the storage compartments at the far-end of the room, "second from the top if I recall." Maggie glanced over her shoulder as Ted knelt to examine the faulty drawer. As soon as he was done fiddling with screws and whatnots she'd catch his eye and make her presence known. She ought to thank him again for coming to her rescue, apologize for Bertha's sharp teeth and report on the jalopy's improved state of health… and perhaps make a few enquires as to the whereabouts of a certain acquaintance of his.

"You know how to dance dontcha?" Clara hissed in Maggie's direction, her lip twisting in pretty mirth.

"Sure I do," Maggie said a little too loudly for Mary's liking. As expected, a curt shushing ensued, followed by the pleasant clinking of Ted's tools.

"I'm not a complete ninny, even if you might think it," Maggie braved a few minutes later.

"Oh yeah?" Clara said, dubious, "I bet."

"I muddle along," Maggie sniffed, "as far as dancing goes." The truth of the matter was she wouldn't know a Rumba or Samba if it hit her square in the face, it was the type of mystery best left to others to sort out. "I can manage a decent foxtrot, besides there's always fun in trying."

"Very trying I'd say," Harriet said.

"But isn't it marvelous? A night out on the boss, it's awful generous don't you think?"

"You got that right," Clara muttered.

"Yeah well I wouldn't mind getting a bit of shut-eye for once," Harriet drawled, "but now I gotta spend the night dragging my fanny around fighting off some sweaty octopus—"

"Octopus!" Maggie guffawed, "why yes—I suppose there's always one or two in the room."

"How bout a dozen?" Harriet countered.

"But what about Walter? He'll protect you from dangerous sea-creatures won't he? I'm terribly eager to meet him."

"Fat chance—"

"Aw quit your hollering Hattie," Clara broke in, scowling at her ungrateful colleague, "boy, what more d'ya want? A night on the town with free hooch and music—*sheesh*."

"What more do I want? Hm. Lets see, well hows about a big, fat pay-rise for starters?"

"Yeah?" Clara said, her voice rising dangerously close to the dreaded Mary threshold, "ask me you oughta be grateful."

"For what? Twenty-two bucks a week?"

"Ugh…" Maggie let out a groan, glaring at the Orphan, "never figured I'd get sick of the sight of blue—it's criminal."

"Ask me green's the pits." Clara stuck out her tongue at the Prince, who whether in the throes of a sword-fight or attending a royal ball was neither expected nor permitted to change his forest-green tights, "red's what gets me going," she purred, "satin—fits me like a glove, you just wait." She wiggled her shoulders in anticipation of Saturday night, "Milt's gonna drop dead when he gets a load of it."

"Then who you gonna marry?" Harriet teased.

"Oh, *real* funny wiseguy."

Maggie dipped her brush and returned to the never-ending iterations of the too-full, too-blue skirt, reminding herself that each brushstroke brought the Orphan closer to glory, a red-carpet event she might even have the pleasure of attending. Perhaps, say, on the arm of a certain Art Schrieber. They were, after all, bound to be pals…if not more. And Clara was quite right. They ought to be grateful for jobs at all.

After a chest-heaving sigh and a shake of her brown curls she returned to the Orphan, who in Maggie's firm opinion ought be ordered by royal decree to swap her skirt with a sensible pair of pants immediately. She slid the brush into the tightest most challenging corner, and, suddenly remembering Ted, turned to the back of the room. But it was too late, the drawer was fixed but Ted had gone.

"Hey where you going?" Harriet said the next day at lunch as Maggie rose from the table.

"Stretching my legs. They'll seize up with all the sitting about."

"You haven't finished your lunch," Harriet eyed Maggie's half-eaten baloney sandwich, "okay if I finish it up?"

"Go right ahead. I've gone off the stuff."

In the space of three weeks baloney wasn't the only thing she'd gone off. Maggie's boredom had extended to hotpot, sausage, chili-beans, and she'd developed the fervent hope that apple-cakes might one day contain at least a trace of their namesake fruit.

"Lucky me," Harriet said as she grabbed the rejected sandwich, "an extra sandwich *and* a dance." Maggie, eager to leave her new friend to her baloney and ungracious thoughts, set off in the direction of progress. Magic was all very well for fairy-tale kingdoms playing host to irritating orphans, but wasting time hoping Art would appear out of nowhere in a puff of smoke was simply foolish.

Her pace quickened and she swung right past Wild Willie, Marley Moose and Bucky Wellhorn, and after another hundred yards or so she arrived. "Here I come," Maggie announced to no-one as the heavy door swung open with barely a squeak. Building A, a clone of the one she planned on leaving as soon as humanly possible, was much as expected, long corridors lined with glass-paneled doors and the same gray, linoleum floor.

But on the walls were portraits of Harley heroes—or in other words, Milt's top men. "John Sciaccia, Jack Bollon, Dirk Nolan," she said, identifying each of the animators as she passed by, "*there you are*," she tutted, waving a finger at Art's oversized face. And, at the end of the passageway, twice the size of his underlings and presiding over them all was their leader—the great and all-powerful Mr Milton Harley. She thrust her face close to his, "make way for the ladies Mr—"

"Maggie?"

She jumped, as though caught in the act of something far more devious than scolding a photograph, "I was just having a word to the boss—"

"Oh?" Ted grinned.

"Letting him know what's what."

"That drawer holding up okay?" he hefted the toolbox, rear-ranging his grip.

"Oh yes. Capital," she frowned, "so you *did* see me, I wasn't sure you had."

"Why yes I…"

"You see I wanted to pass on the good news, Bertha's fit as a fiddle—but by the time I looked up you'd gone, disappeared into thin air like Houdini, unless I fell asleep or was hypnotized by my brush, which I believe might be quite possible—" she mimed the action, turning her head from side to side as though under a spell, "I tell you too long down at Paint and Ink does strange things to a girl."

"Sure. Well it needed a new runner so I patched it up."

"What?"

"The drawer, should hold up fine now."

"Marvelous…perhaps you could see to the door as well, stop the squeaking so we can sneak out when Mary nods off. Not that she does very often, or at all, but Hattie swears it happens—or happened…once." She searched the hallway for a clock. Only sixteen minutes left to get back to jail, "where you headed? Another bust cupboard?"

"Camera-room."

"Oh? So it's not just hinges and things?"

"Nope."

"Not the same old thing day in, day out? Lucky you."

"Nope." His torso twisted as a group of men approached, a small herd bound together in lockstep.

"Well, thank-you again Ted," Maggie said, anxious to complete her mission.

"Would you like to uh—come take a look?" He rubbed his chin, nervous.

"What? The camera-room?"

"Uh-huh. Take a peek round, see how things work."

"I'd like that very much, very much indeed. But I'm trying to find Mr Schrieber you see, for advice, and I don't have much time." Maggie nodded her acknowledgement as the men passed by.

"Playing grease monkey again?" one of them called out.

"That's right," Ted hefted the box again and turned to Maggie, "he's upstairs, Room A3."

She peered through the glass before rapping on the door. "Come in if you're good-looking," came a jocular voice from within. She entered, suddenly nervous among the world-renowned artists, Milton's top men.

"So this is where the fellas live?" she said before introducing herself.

"I'm Jack, how do you do." The other man, John Sciaccia, regarded her cooly.

"Yes I just met you all in the hallway, but don't be offended, I'm looking for someone else." She glanced about the room anxiously. The place was a good deal messier than Paint and Ink. Evidently less wrangling took place here than in Sergeant Mary's kingdom of order and precision...here a fledgeling animator might find the room to spread her wings and fly. "Mr Schrieber, is he here?"

"The one and only," Jack muttered, gesturing to a desk set a little apart from the rest.

"But I'm honored to meet you all," Maggie added, smiling brightly as Art looked up from his work and slipped a pencil behind his ear.

"So you managed to hunt me down?"

"It wasn't so difficult," she said, examining a sequence of drawings tacked to a board, a cheeky raccoon riding the leg of a benign-faced ogre, "my—who's this darling? We haven't seen him down at Paint and Ink yet."

"Like him?" Art removed the pencil and tapped it in the cup of his hand.

"Boy do I ever—he's terrific."

"Least someone round here sees sense."

"Oh?"

"Uncle Milt ain't so sure," he scowled, "odds are Mr Raccoon'll wind up on the cutting-room floor, way things are headed."

"Well I can't for the life of me see why. Uncle Milt must have rocks in his head," she surmised.

"Wouldn't go around calling him that. Say, I forgot your name."

"Oh..." her face fell, "it's Maggie."

"Sure. Maggie, I remember. The wannabe animator."

"Wannabe?" Maggie snorted at the thought. She had nothing

whatever in common with garden-variety Hollywood air-heads living off pipe-dreams and the kindness of strangers—or strange men as was often the case, "that's not how I see it."

"Oh? How do you see it? You done with Paint and Ink yet?"

She caught the inside of her cheek in her teeth, a habit retained from childhood, back when her mother had still been around to teach the washing of hands, crossing of legs and all the pleases and thank yous. "No, not yet, not done with Paint and Ink," she said, recovered from her offense, "only a million, billion trillion more blue skirts to go…or something like that."

"Don't blame me, the Orphan's John's doing. I'm the ogre and he wears trousers, and short ones at that."

"Well Clara complains about his warts. *Wart-head* she calls him, not very inventive I'm afraid." Art leaned back in his chair and crossed his arms, regarding her with some bemusement.

"What can I do for you Maggie? To what do I owe the pleasure?"

"Do?" her eyebrows arched in surprise, "but don't you recall? You said you'd lend a hand, help out with my squirrel. As a matter of fact you said you'd be delighted, so here I am—come to remind you."

"Always happy to be reminded, specially when it comes to being delighted."

"My squirrel." She took the three-inch pad from her pocket and handed it over, and as Art flipped the pages the two-dimensional critter sprang to life, leaping from stage left to right. "See…? *Here*—no, start over." Maggie, watching over his shoulder, held her breath as he flipped again, "stop—just *there*. Now do I need more frames or are there too many already?" She searched the expert's face, trying but failing to read his thoughts.

"Not bad," he said finally, opening the booklet near the start again, "but you got too-big a jump here, see? Right at the get-go."

"Can't say I blame her—it is the hardest part wouldn't you say, getting things started?" She slipped the pad back in her pocket, "but then when the ball's rolling you can't stop it can you? Can't give up till you get it right…is what I'm getting at."

"Whats you put in is whats you get out," Art said, his tone slightly mocking.

"Yes that's right…" Maggie, unsure of his meaning, shifted uncomfortably from foot to foot, "will I see you on Saturday? At the Palomar?"

"Bosses orders, but I'll give you fair warning—I got two left feet okay?"

"Then we'll have a *bunch* of left feet—four of them in total— with me thrown into the deal…"

"Sure, should be a real show." He reached over, plucked a thumb-tack from the board and removed one of the raccoons, "here, a souvenir, hot off the press."

"But…won't you need it?" Joy surged in her heart as she held the sketch with great reverence.

"Plenty more where that came from."

"A souvenir huh?" she smirked, "well it's been a swell visit Mr Schrieber, but I'll have you know I plan on immigrating here permanently."

"So you said. Well, good luck getting that passport."

She rushed back to Paint and Ink, pressing the precious sketch to her heart. Although a little tightly-wound, with the aid of a smile Art really was quite the dish…and such darling little teeth, small and even—a bit like his raccoon.

Her cheeks flushed at the warm and exciting thoughts flooding her body and mind. In all her twenty-seven and a half years Maggie had never truly felt the sweet sting of Cupid's arrow. But now it seemed the cherubic Angel had either sharpened his flint or improved his wonky aim.

Chapter Four

————————

*B*unker Hill was quite a hill. Bertha groaned and chugged up the steep incline to 109 Greening street. A thick, gnarled vine snaked through a fence in danger of toppling over at any moment, and weeds sprang from every available crack and patch. In short, the place looked altogether run-down.

Maggie pulled up at the curb and set the brake with a firm tug. The last thing she needed was a runaway car, especially as Ted's man at Bingleys had recommended seeing to the lever—not to mention the engine thingamajig wearing thin as a beggar's leg, a valve or piston or some such thing.

"Hey-ho!" Maggie called out. Harriet jumped from the porch of the rambling Victorian mansion, ran down the steps and wrestled with the passenger door. "So this is your famous hill?" Maggie said, keeping a steady pressure on the brake as they descended, "is it a family home?"

"If it is they oughta be shot," Harriet mumbled. She scowled and rifled through her handbag.

"I suppose the bedrooms are upstairs?" Maggie went on, swerving to avoid a great crack in the road, "the view oughta be terrific."

"Why there you are you little sucker—" Harriet twisted the end of the wayward lipstick, applied pink to her lips and checked the result in her compact, "that'll have to do."

In no time at all they arrived downtown. "Last time I shopped at Bullocks was before I got hitched," Harriet revealed as they passed a jewelry store promising the finest in gold and silver bands. A woman left the store, ecstatic and admiring her newly-encircled finger, her fiance proud as punch at her side. "Good luck," Harriet yelled out cheekily as they pulled up at the department store on seventh and Broadway, "you'll sure as hell need it."

With Harriet in tow Maggie lead the way in, and after a few false starts ending in detours through footwear and lingerie, the giggling pair arrived at evening-wear.

"Oo-la-la! This little number ring your bell, ma'am?" Having found the most ostentatious dress on the rack, Harriet swung the glittering configuration from side to side like a flag at a bullfight. She sized it up against her friend.

"You gotta be kidding!" Maggie recoiled in horror.

"What's the problem? Little too Clara for you?" They exchanged wry smiles and Maggie marched on, determined to follow Milt's orders and arrive at the Palomar dressed to the nines before nine.

"That's more like it," she rifled through a rack of dresses and found a gorgeous satin in soft green, "and on sale—fifty percent off."

"Now you got the right idea."

Maggie slipped the satin from the rack and flipped it over to inspect the back, or what was left of it, which wasn't much at all. "Running short on material I guess," Harriet quipped.

"Someone slipped with the scissors," Maggie said, all the while wondering if the thing wasn't perfectly suited to a fancy night out, besides, she was sure Art wouldn't mind a bit of skimping as far as material went, "don't get me wrong, I'm all for scooped backs, but this one's a little *too* scoopy."

"Quit fooling around—" Harriet snatched the dress away and called for assistance. "Don't mind her," she told the shopgirl, "she likes it, just won't say so is all."

"Oughta reel in an octopus or two," Harriet said a few minutes later as Maggie stepped out from the changing-room.

"Oh," Maggie faltered, now unsure.

"Won't stand a chance with that on." Harriet, fingering a fur draped about the shoulders of a fashionably-sloped mannequin, eyed her friend slyly.

"Who?"

"Aw—don't act dumb. *Art.*"

"I suppose he is rather handsome," she smoothed the material at her waist and turned to examine the back.

"So you won't mind if he gets a little fresh then?"

"Well…" Maggie wavered as she admired herself in the mirror. Pink rushed to her cheeks, augmenting the overall effect. "No," she decided finally, "I guess not."

A bow of winking lights signaled into the night and Maggie, her eyes darting like a bird, searched for Harriet outside the Palomar. Her plan to escort her friend to the compulsory shindig had been scuttled by Bertha's unfortunate death, and the old jalopy's sad, rusted hulk had been hauled away outside of Bullocks—not by Ted's man from Bingleys but an equally nice one from a garage not fifty yards from the final hurrah.

Maggie rubbed her arms under the ermine cloak and fastened the clasp. The shopgirl at Bullocks had been very effective with her cajoling and Maggie had at last conceded, it *would* go swimmingly with just about anything in a closet, especially the daring dress that according to Harriet would render Mr Schrieber defenseless.

Maggie frowned in distaste. The idea Art might succumb too thoroughly to her charms was more than a little off-putting.

There was nothing attractive about a man suddenly struck dumb by love, and getting stuck with another Harold Trumble didn't bear thinking about.

Poor old Harold. She winced at the memory. The awkward stroll in a not-quite-private-enough nook in Central Park, the sight of the poor man sweating and perched on one unsteady knee, steeling himself for the home-run, his face crumpled in terror from the force of apparent, undying love.

She supposed there'd been some encouragement leading up to it all. They'd gotten a little friendly once or twice, held hands at the movies, romantic ones full of slush and unreasonable swooning. Not the type of film she liked at all. And that was precisely the problem, she and Harold hadn't a jot in common except fathers who worked for important government-men. "Oh Harold," she'd said for want of anything better, averting her eyes as he'd scrambled to his feet, "do let's sit down and talk things over." And by the time they'd decided on the best sycamore-shaded bench to do just that, Harold had thankfully come to his senses and accorded with the unspoken—there really was nothing more to be said on the subject.

In fact, Maggie mused, love was rather a silly business, but Art was no Harold Trumble and wouldn't flop about swooning at the slightest provocation. *He* was a man who could defeat an entire artillery of dresses, no matter how much material went missing.

She grinned at the thought, dipping her cheek in the delicious nest of fur under her chin. "I made it," Harriet panted, just as Clara came upon them as well—dressed to the tens in all her red, svelte glory. Clara twirled, regarding her colleagues with a look approaching disgust.

"What you doing all the ways back here?"

"Having a smoke, you mind?" Harriet glared at the blood-red bombshell and lit her Lucky Strike, steadying one trembling hand with the other.

"Say—how you like it? Huh?" Clara twirled again, in case they hadn't noticed.

"Sure is, ah…shiny," Harriet said with a smirk. Clara, anxious, took out her compact and checked her face.

"Shiny—?"

"Not your nose."

"Sparkly, she means," Maggie interjected, "a real star."

"You bet I am…all the same, while in Rome."

After applying more powder Clara led the way into the foyer, swaying her show-stopping figure and scanning the room for her octopus of choice. "Would you look at that!" Maggie whooped, agape at the chandelier, monstrous yet marvelous, a cluster of glass drops descending from the heavens in pendulous tiers, fracturing into tinier versions of itself as it hovered over the marble floor.

"That's Hollywood for ya," Harriet said as Clara's dress got to work immediately, heads turning like clowns at a fairground.

"Walter couldn't come?" Maggie said, wondering when she might finally meet Harriet's mysterious husband.

"Didn't ask." She ripped the top from another pack of Lucky Strikes, "want one?"

"No, thank you."

"Wouldn't come even if I did." She tapped her cigarette unnecessarily in an ashtray mounted on a brass lady with one naked breast.

"Doesn't like dancing I suppose?"

"Nope. Loves dancing. And music. Matter of fact he goes on about it till the cows come home."

"Then why isn't he here?"

"Put it down to bad blood," she leaned her hip into Maggie's thigh, "look who's here…your long-haired octopus."

Maggie's heart lurched, or leapt, she wasn't sure which, but one thing was certain—Art was fast approaching, his body turning this way and that as he wove through the swelling crowd. And what's more, he scrubbed up very well indeed, the unruly hair soothed into calmer waves than usual, his daring zoot-suit setting him apart from the more conventional types. It was the type of man Art was, Maggie decided, worthy of special attention.

"Surprised they let you in," Harriet said, giving him the once-over.

"Evening ladies," he grinned and turned his attention to Maggie, "ready to kick up some dust?"

"I'd be delighted," Maggie said in a voice slightly higher than the one she knew as her own.

"Soon as they get done with this goddamned swing."

"Yes, swing," Maggie echoed, unsure of the basis of his complaint. As far as she could make out the goddamned swing was doing a capital job of luring dancers to their feet.

"Let him warm up a bit," Harriet advised, "he's a grump."

"That's right," Art shrugged, moving his shoulders in a slow circle as though preparing for a fight or some kind of race. He raised his glass and drained his drink in one fell swoop. "How's that squirrel of yours shaping up?" He turned to Harriet, "you seen her squirrel?"

"Course, we've all seen it," Harriet rolled her eyes.

"Not everyone," Maggie frowned at her drink, all the while thinking it a miracle Harriet's eyes hadn't shot out of her head, what with all the winding they did. "Squirrel's awful curious you see, dying to get acquainted."

"A schmoozer," Art concluded.

"Knows what she wants is all."

"This one hunted me down, she tell you that?"

Maggie felt Art's shoulder brush against hers as he shifted to get a better view of the disappointing musicians. "Good heavens, hunted?" Maggie scoffed, "why I'm no predator, all I did was knock on the door and make myself known—I hardly chased you about at gun-point."

"A gun might come in handy tonight," Harriet noted. She drew back a lungful of smoke and picked something from her teeth.

"Yep, the talk of the town, you are." Art's brows rose suggestively.

"Am I?"

"Getting quite the reputation."

Maggie, sipping her apple-flavored cocktail with perhaps a little too much vigor, began to feel a little heated. So far the courage to fling off her outer-skin and reveal the eye-catching scoop beneath had not yet struck. She looked over at Milton's ring-side table and wished she were more like Clara. More brazen, more…thrust-forward. "Why I don't mind reputations, so long as they're for the right things."

"And what might they be?" Art regarded her with look that wasn't quite friendly.

"Hard work for starters. Talent. Determination."

"That include wandering off from your station?" he demanded, a smile playing at his lips, "did sergeant what's her name give you a hall-pass?"

"Sergeant Mary," Harriet interjected.

"Yeah. Sergeant Mary. That's the one. I've a mind to rat on you Maggie, can't have you costing Uncle Milt time and money."

"Yeah, no slacking off or he won't get that second mansion in Beverly Hills," Harriet laughed ruefully, "poor fella."

"It was lunch time," Maggie sniffed, "there's no law against exploring, and I wouldn't dream of wasting Mr Harley's time. No, we're all in this together, getting our Orphan up on the big screen…prancing through the forest and whatever else she gets up to—"

"Bet she won't go hunting with a gun," Harriet said.

"Not unless she gets a hall-pass," Art said with a wink.

"No siree. Our Little Orphan gets herself a bood-i-ful dress and goes to the ball. Yep. Comes up roses every time."

"Yeah all hunky dory," Art scoffed.

"Oh no…" Maggie's face fell, "not a *ball* dress as well? Better not be blue—"

"But we're in this together aren't we? Making sacrifices and all?" Harriet caught Art's eye and grinned.

"Relax, it's pink," Art said, staring into the distance.

"Thank goodness for that, I've been on a terribly bland diet of D16."

"Got something against D16?" Art said, affecting outrage.

"Why not at all, every color is equal in my books…I'm very progressive you know."

"That so…? Glad to hear it."

The band struck up a jazzier tune, a decent enough compromise, Art surmised, if they weren't to have the real thing. He grabbed Maggie's hand and led her to the dance-floor, and, to Maggie's surprise, their contingent of left feet managed quite nicely together. In fact they seemed to be getting the hang of the foxtrot or whatever it was they were making a fist of, and when she removed her pelt and revealed her scoop to whomsoever cared to admire it, Art hadn't dropped dead at all.

"Miss Goldilocks got her claws in already," Art yelled above the noise. He nodded at Clara and Milton, zipping past in a sure-footed whirlwind of white and red.

"Another predator I'm afraid. I suppose if anyone's dangerous she is."

"We're on safari."

"On the wild savanna," Maggie agreed, a little anxious about the position of her hand. Ought she rest it on the nape of his neck or keep it resting primly on his rather wiry shoulder? "And Uncle Milt's the lion. The biggest prize of all. Perhaps I oughta loan Clara my gun."

"I'll load the bullets myself," Art said, his eyes narrowed.

"You don't meant that?" She regarded him with some alarm, "do you?"

"What do you think?"

"I'm sure I don't know you well enough to say…"

"Yeah well Clara don't need a gun to get what she wants, that's for sure."

He pulled her closer, narrowly avoiding a collision with a couple marooned in the centre of the floor. Maggie tensed. "But enough about guns, let's talk about more interesting weapons," she said, adjusting to the more intimate embrace he'd initiated, his hand spread at the small of her back, "pencils for example."

"Not much you can say about a pencil," he laughed, displaying his neat little teeth, "about seven inches long. Pointed at one end, looks a bit like a twig."

"A rather straight twig I'd say—but what type is best for the job?"

"Depends."

"But what do *you* use?"

"2B's standard," he said, clearly distracted.

"Not too dark?"

"Listen—you gonna spend the whole night gabbing about pencils?" He exhaled dramatically and shook his head.

"I'm not gabbing…*or* yammering for that matter." She tightened her grip as he silenced her with a sudden twirl, "look out—!"

They swerved but it was too late. Maggie let out a cry as glasses toppled and drink spilled, surprising and dismaying the occupants of Milton's ring-side table. She scrambled to her feet, apologizing effusively and mopping the tablecloth with an over-starched napkin. "Jack, I'm awful sorry, here—let me get you another drink."

Just then Art pulled her back into the mass of swirling bodies and there was no time to make amends. She craned her neck, gazing back at the scene, Jack and John and various other members of Harley's inner circle carrying on as they had before. "But we ought to see to more drinks—"

"They can fend for themselves," Art said tightly as the song came to an end and a slower one began, "see enough of their ugly mugs as it is." He released Maggie from his arms and plucked a cigarette from a silver case, "but be my guest, go right ahead."

"Oh…sure," Maggie said, forcing a smile.

"Besides, folks'll think I'm soft if I don't spread myself round." He waved at Bert, standing at the bar and saluting with his drink.

"Well. Can't have you ruining your reputation can we?" Maggie said with as much cheer as she could muster, "but you'll find me later on won't you? For another shot at the foxtrot or whatnot?" She rubbed her leg and squared him a direct look.

"Sure."

"Or how about supper sometime? There's only so many hamburgers a girl can stomach, besides I need a local to get me acquainted—Harriet's always got some excuse."

"I'm from Missouri."

"But you eat don't you?"

"Okay, okay, you got me there. But promise me one thing."

"Sure."

"Don't bring that gun of yours."

"Wouldn't dream of it," Maggie quipped, her spirits rising. "I'll bring a pencil—a sharp, twiggy one. Next week?"

"Sure. Next week, why not."

She fought her way back to the upset table to finish what she'd started, replace spilt drinks or mop up messes. "Sorry about that," she yelled above the band, at last a tune she recognized—*Music Maestro, Please.*

"Well, if it ain't miss hi-hat," Clara called out.

"Hi-hat?" Maggie frowned.

"Oh quit takin y'rself so serious," Clara said, raising her glass in a cheer, "to The Hot Spots!"

Milton, a picture of sartorial splendor in a white box-shouldered suit, eyed Clara fondly and turned to Maggie, his face ruddy with bonhomie. "Don't just stand there, sit down—for God's sake where's your drink?"

"I suppose it's drunk."

"Easy fix." Milton gestured to the champagne resting in a silver ice-bucket, "get the girl a drink."

"Yes boss," Clara said with good-humor.

"I really oughtn't—one accident is enough," Maggie said, accepting the glass despite herself.

"Come now, take the weight off," Jack said, poaching a chair from a nearby table and ordering her to sit.

"Thank you. I'm sorry about before. Did we break anything?"

"*You* didn't." Jack cast a meaningful look at Milton.

"Say, where's your fella?" Clara shouted over the booming horns, "he get spooked or someth'n?" She laughed and crossed her eyes, somehow maintaining her loveliness throughout.

"Spooked?" Maggie glanced over her shoulder at the bar, "no, just retired, or at least for the time being…I'm sure we'll take another shot at it…later on." Her brow furrowed and she wondered who else Art felt obliged to share himself with lest he be seen as soft, "and if he doesn't come back of his own accord I'll be obliged to hunt him down," she announced boldly, "we're on safari you see."

"Atta girl," Clara lifted her glass to make another toast, "to safaris!"

"She got a mind to be an animator, this one," Milton announced to the table of elites. Jack, greatly amused, snorted loudly.

"But there ain't no lady animators."

"And not too long ago there were no automobiles," Maggie reminded him. He pushed his glass roughly and stared at his

plate. "You don't want us going back to horses and carts do you?"
She sipped her champagne, the bubbles tickling her nose, her eyes
filling with tears from the sting. "I'm quite settled on the matter—
I won't stand in the way of progress, social or otherwise, and I
hope none of you men intend to either. No sense clinging to old
ways." She peeked at Milton, still amiable, it seemed, to the idea
of a lady animator, "I understand there's a woman in Building A
already—perhaps she'd like a companion?"

"That's right," Milton said as Clara fussed with his lapel,
"Ruby Meiche. Heads up costume design—but you ladies know
about fashion, in the blood."

"Sure is," Clara nodded.

"And other things," Maggie insisted, "drawing, for instance."

"Ouch!" Jack blew on his hands as if they'd suddenly burst
into flames, "we got ourselves a live-wire here."

"That's right," Maggie smiled sweetly, "I won't quit."

"How about it fellas?" Milton raised a brow and chuckled,
"any objections to a filly joining the gang? Never know, might be
a position sooner than you think."

The men exchanged wry smiles as Maggie latched on to the
incredible carrot dangling in front of her face and clung on tight.
Position? Had Milton really said that…? Here she was in the heart
of the action with the door wide-open and an invitation to enter.
"Oh and that reminds me," Maggie said, flushed with joy and
emboldened by drink, "I must have a word with you Mr Harley."

"Milton—"

"Milton. About the raccoon, Art's raccoon."

"What about it?" He regarded her warily through plumes of
smoke and flicked his cigarette.

"Well," Maggie ventured, "I understand you don't approve of
him so much."

"So Schrieber's got you doing his bidding has he?"

"Oh not at all, *no*," Maggie scowled, greatly offended by the thought, "I'm acting quite on my own behalf, and it's for the good of the studio I say it you see, *our* studio—Mr Raccoon can't end up on the cutting-room floor—no no—he deserves a fighting chance, *more* than a fighting chance…" Her heart constricted at the sight of Milton's sudden transformation, the frozen pose and lips pressed in a thin line, anger snaking to the surface like a lizard about to strike a fly.

"I'd advise you to keep to your *own* business, if you don't mind," he growled.

"Shh—" Clara hissed, her warning too late.

"But I'm only trying to help—" Maggie began as Milton shoved his chair back and pulled Clara to her feet.

"Hold on there big boy." Clara emptied her drink, smacked her lips and sailed away in Milton's arms.

Maggie, greatly sobered by the outburst and eager to make inroads with the gang, turned to John and Jack. She leaned in to catch the gist of their conversation, but if Milt's men were talking shop she couldn't make heads or tails of it.

"Won't you excuse me?"

She stood abruptly, searching among the sea of animated faces as the horns blared on. The band, sweating in their suits, showed no sign of slowing down—the night certainly wasn't about to end any time soon. She released her cheek from the prison of her teeth, suddenly exhausted, her shoulders slumped… surely Art had proved his hardness to his pals by now. She rubbed her forehead, her brow knitting in pain, a headache would be next, and she really ought to find Harriet.

"There you are," Maggie muttered as she spied the zoot-suited man at the far end of the bar. She fought through the crowd, tapped on his shoulder and he turned. "Oh, I beg your pardon, I'm looking for a friend, Art Schrieber? You look quite similar from the back—"

"Well ain't you a sweetie-patootie," the man leered, his gaze sliding south to settle on her chest. She recoiled, suddenly suffocated by the noise, the smoke, the writhing, close crowd—and the red-faced man with bad manners wasn't helping any.

"Ring-a-*ding-ding*," said his equally unsteady friend as she fastened another of the fur's clasps.

"Care for dance?" the first one said, leaning over to shout in her ear.

"No thank you." Maggie stiffened, "but isn't the band terrific? The Hot Spots. Mr Harley had them drop everything to be here you know."

"Oh sure, the guy's a real swell." He listed forward and grabbed at her waist.

"Hey Mr—get your meat hooks off!" Harriet, appearing miraculously from out of nowhere, wrenched his arm away, "don't you got something better to do?"

"Aw—now don't get all snarled up about it," he yelled nastily as Harriet and Maggie retreated to find shelter. "Go on—scram, silly cows."

"Well I never," Maggie exclaimed, appalled by the man's manners.

"Forget it, the guy's ossified…and you don't look so hot your-self," Harriet eyed Maggie with a grin, "don't know bout you, but I'm beat."

"Guess we oughta pack it in."

"Home?"

"Home," Maggie agreed.

"If we hurry along we'll catch the last trolley."

"Don't be silly, we'll get a cab," Maggie said, re-pinning her hat. "Where's Clara? To say goodbye."

"If you say so," Harriet grumbled.

"Come on. Won't take a minute."

They squeezed through the rowdy mass to the ring-side table, Maggie still on the lookout for Art and figuring he must have hardened to a statue by now. At least that would explain why he hadn't sought her out. Or perhaps he'd shot through after failing to track her down, or had the relentless swing driven him away in the end…?

"He's not such a bad dancer—except our little crash," Maggie confided as she and Harriet came upon Clara, now atop Milton's lap and whispering something delicious in his rather large ear.

The table was positively chock-a-block now, chairs squeezed in at all angles to accommodate newcomers gravitating to the star attraction. Maggie nodded to Jack, seemingly engrossed in a scintillating conversation with a woman she recognized from Paint and Ink. And, standing behind Milton—evidently waiting for Clara to finish with the boss's ear so he might have a word in it, was Ted.

Maggie blinked, slightly taken aback by the sight of him dressed to the nines and looking rather more handsome than she'd remembered. It hadn't occurred to her that Milton's invitation would extend to the lesser tiers of the Harley family, to drawer-fixers or mechanics or whatever it was Ted did. "Ted—" she called out, her hands cupped to her mouth.

"You're kidding," Clara yelled as soon as she saw the ominous sign of her friends standing by, "don't tell me you're gonna split? *Already?*"

"Uh-huh. Shipping out," Harriet confirmed.

"Suit y'self, I'm staying put till the boss packs it in." She turned to Milton and purred, "gonna take me home big boy?"

"You bet," he said, nuzzling her splendid neck.

"Oh you *will*, will you—" Clara slapped him playfully and he tightened his grip about her waist. "That's better," she said, settling into his embrace, "nice and cosy."

"A–hoy there!" Maggie called out again. This time Ted looked up. A smile broke across his face and he launched into action, straightening his lanky frame and squeezing through bodies until he reached her side.

"I was hoping to see you," he said, already blushing.

"Here I am," she smiled away weariness, "a little under the

weather but nothing serious. Too much bubbly stuff—I'll be right as rain tomorrow."

"Are you—" he cleared his throat and gestured to the dance-floor, "dancing?"

"I made a fist of it earlier, only a few bruises…but I'm afraid we're off."

"Okay," he said, a little downcast.

"Yes it's bedtime for this clumsy hoofer. Sorry. Perhaps another time."

"Coming?" Harriet, impatient to set sail, nodded at Ted and turned to leave.

"If we don't leave soon our coach'll turn into a pumpkin," Maggie said with a grin. She narrowed her eyes, "you *are* familiar with the story?" He stood, wordless, a blush creeping from neck to cheek. "And Bertha couldn't come to the ball poor thing—in fact she won't be going anywhere from now on I'm afraid."

"Come on—" Harriet tugged her arm, "there's cabs out front."

"Well…goodnight."

"Hold up," he said, touching her arm gently, "how about I give you a ride?"

"Oh…" Maggie frowned, "would you? But you won't mind taking the both of us? It's rather a drive."

"Nope. Plenty of gas. Where you headed?"

"We'll take a cab," Harriet hissed in Maggie's ear.

"She's Bunker Hill and I'm Huntington Park," Maggie said, ignoring the elbow in her ribs.

"Back in a minute, wait there." Ted made his way back to Milton and leaned in to get his attention. The boss nodded, then returned to the business of rescuing Clara as she slid ingloriously from his lap to the floor.

"What's the matter?" Maggie asked as Harriet regarded her with annoyance. But it was too late to discover the source of her agitation, Ted was back, his face bright and eyes shining. He thrust his hands in his pockets and shouldered through the heaving crowd, ushering the women into the night.

"Ah—that's more like it." Maggie sucked in cool air, her eyes closed with pleasure, "isn't air wonderful?" She opened her eyes to see Ted's rather startling ones looking right back.

"Uh-huh," he smiled, "sure is."

"Yeah. Terrific." Harriet lit another cigarette as the attendant arrived with Ted's car.

"Here she is." He tapped the hood of an expensive-looking vehicle and opened the door for his passengers, "after you ladies."

"Gee…not bad," Maggie whistled, bouncing on the well-sprung seat as Harriet, immediately slumping in a corner, started to yawn.

"Where to first?"

"Oh I don't mind," Maggie breezed.

"I'll take your friend then," he decided as they took off in the slick machine.

Harriet, her head lolling against Maggie's tall shoulder, soon dozed off and they drove in silence through the streets of downtown Los Angeles, past bright theater lights and noisy patrons carousing the streets. "You know I feel like we're flying above it all on a magic carpet." Maggie unpinned her hat and the wind lifted her hair in a halo of dark brown. She glanced at Ted, his hand flopped casually over the wheel, totally at ease in his role of master of machine, "I saw it in a movie and said to myself—now that's just how I'd like to travel. Have you seen *Knights of the Desert*?"

"Can't say as I have."

"Oh it's marvelous. You oughta see it right away," Maggie said, hoping for a little small-talk to pass the time, "adventure movies are the best sort—oh, except for cartoons of course, what type of movie do you go in for?"

"Well," he began uncertainly.

"What about gangsters? Guns and criminals and the like?"

"They're all right," he managed.

"This street's quicker," Harriet said, stirring from her slumber and pointing left. They slowed and turned into the side-street.

"Isn't the car marvelous?" Maggie said before her friend had the chance to doze off again, "as quiet as a mouse compared to Bertha," she sighed sadly, "poor old thing."

"Terrific," Harriet yawned.

"Belongs to the boss," Ted revealed, glancing at Maggie as they waited for the signal to turn green.

"Does she?" Maggie said, distracted by thoughts drifting very much in the direction of Art, "why it's awful kind of him…"

They reached Bunkers Hill and Maggie shook her friend gently, "wake up sleepyhead."

"Wha—?" Harriet gasped, her eyes flying open.

"You've arrived safe and sound thanks to our chauffeur."

"Thank you," Harriet said tightly. She stepped out of the car and ran up the steps to the unlit porch.

"Too late for a nose-around now." Maggie gazed at the rickety house, eerie in the dead of night, "she never invites me in. You see her husband's out of work and I don't suppose he likes keeping house much, poor Harriet gets home to a mess most days," she explained, doubting Ted would have much to say on the subject, "and there's such an awful lot to be done when no-one does it for you…food, for instance, do you know I haven't touched my cooker once since I got here—not a once." She managed a tired laugh, closed her eyes, and let silence descend.

"Just up here a bit," Maggie said some time later. "Thank you. It's been a lovely ride, quite…relaxing."

"You hungry?" Ted asked suddenly. He shifted gear and turned into her street.

"Oh no—not at all…"

Maggie held her breath, fearing he might invite her to a late-night supper where she'd have to do all the talking. "All that champagne I'm afraid there's no room…" The engine dropped to a low rumble as they neared her apartment block, "well…good-night." She flashed Ted a smile and stepped out of the car, "and you'll thank Mr Harley for the loan of his car won't you?"

Chapter Five

The motor-coach stopped high on the plateau and Maggie gathered her belongings, the large sketchpad and tin of pencils she'd brought for her adventure. According to Harriet and just about everyone she'd met in Los Angeles, she simply must take a hike in Griffith Park.

"What time's the last coach?" she asked the driver as she disembarked.

"Seven o'clock."

"Don't want to get stranded—die of thirst with no one finding me for days."

"Watch out for them critters," he warned, "most of 'em got rabies."

"You don't say…?" Maggie frowned as the driver gave her the once-over.

"You all alone?"

"Just little ole me and my pencils," Maggie patted the unopened pack of 2Bs she'd rushed out to buy that morning, "and coffee and crackers, it's all I need for a day on my own."

"Whatever you say lady."

She might see a fox, or a wolf, or even a skunk…was it true they smelt so bad? She headed to a downhill trail, and, reading the sign at the entrance, felt a sudden rush of gratitude for their president.

This trail was constructed as part of the Works Progress Administration…

Without Mr. Roosevelt's New Deal the country would be a mess, or more of a mess than it was already—which was quite a mess for some, most notably the refugees fleeing the dustbowl from out east, desperate, hungry families piled into cars overflowing with worldly possessions.

She shifted the pack on her back and adjusted her new hat. The shop-girl at Bullocks had insisted the accessory was both practical and fashionable. She wouldn't look out of place, Maggie soon realized, spotting a women wearing a similar if not identical one to her own. She pulled off her sweater, tied it about her waist and started down the trail, her sneaks padding tracks in the powdery dust as she searched for inspiration in the brushy woodland.

The trail became steeper, more wooded, and at last there came the faint sound of trickling water, a tiny stream at the bottom of the canyon, the perfect spot for an adventurous squirrel. She unstrapped her pack and made a seat of a rock, settling in and demolishing a few crackers as a leaf floated by in the tiny waterway. It stopped, suddenly trapped by a half-submerged twig, but as Maggie reached over to assist its passage, the leaf broke free and surged on. "Off you go," she murmured as the vessel continued its hazardous journey, a tiny boat sailing valiantly to who-knew where.

Inspired, she opened her pencils and began sketching. Her squirrel might be a passenger on that leaf-boat, relaxing after an arduous day of sailing, paws linked behind her head and gazing up at the sky. And a cloud might waft in from the left, lingering, dancing—morphing into curled shapes. Then…danger—a half-submerged turtle rising from the depths, a monstrous wave erupting in its wake…

She slapped a mosquito needling her ankle, tucked her legs away from the sun's rays and continued…And, when the cloud was done with its peacocking, it would take the shape of a love-heart, and after that, the adorable face of a sweetheart…and who better to fit that role than Art's darling raccoon?

"No skunks or wolves," Maggie informed her father later that day, having returned unmolested from Griffith Park. She cradled the receiver to her ear and finished the job of smoothing cold-cream on her tender, sun-burned shin, "didn't miss the bus or get rabies."

"Very clever."

She smiled at the sound of her father's high-pitched chuckle. He always approved it seemed, no matter what she did or said. "How you getting along with your painting?"

"I've marvelous news Paps!"

"Oh?"

"There's a position in animation—or will be—and I'm getting a bunch of advice about pencils and the like, and Mr Harley's a terrific dancer—spent a *fortune* on the band, flew them in from Florida just for us…but he doesn't like squirrels much, or raccoons for that matter. But he'll come round when he sees what she's been up to."

"Up to no good I bet—"

"What do you mean no good? Squirrel's had a mighty adventure—she deserves to be commended not scolded. *And* she's made a new friend…a darling raccoon as a matter of fact."

"Raccoon? No better than vermin…no rabies I hope?"

"I should say not," Maggie said, warmth flooding her cheeks.

"I've wired money for your automobile. But find some fella to steer you in the right direction this time will you?"

"You have my absolute and solemn word on it."

She returned to her chair and took up her tools, sharpening

the pencil that had shrunk to less than half its size in what seemed like no time at all. The 2Bs were just right, soft enough but not so soft they smudged or messed up the paper. She adjusted the curve of a sturdy leg braced to fend off a turtle-induced wave, "Uncle Milt'll see what he's missing," Maggie murmured to her cartoon companion, suddenly realizing she'd need Art's permission if their furry critters were to be sweethearts.

She felt a little thrill as her thoughts turned to Art. More than a week had passed since they'd made their crashing debut at the Palomar. She eyed the telephone that refused to ring and felt certain he'd make good on his promise and take her to supper soon, her number *was* listed…she'd called herself to make sure.

Chapter Six

When the sergeant began her fidgeting then something was surely up. Mary, stood at the helm of the room, fussed with her blouse and addressed the women under her strict supervision.

"What's eating her?" Clara hissed.

"Ladies," Mary began, brushing her skirt with a flick of the wrist, "your full attention please—if you don't mind." Maggie looked up from the latest iteration of the Orphan's twirling skirt and let out a sigh. Couldn't she and the Prince have a little rest and sit under a tree for a bit, take a nap instead of prancing and dancing about? "It's all here on the schedule," Mary held up a sheet of paper then clipped among desks to distribute the document, "time to double-down girls."

"What the heck's this?" Harriet mumbled, scowling at the list of names and corresponding numbers.

"Beats me," Maggie said.

"We need to keep a tight ship ladies."

"Already do—" came a low voice behind Maggie. It was Dora, who, much like Harriet, tended to a state of disgruntlement when it came to their famous employer.

"A new system," Mary cleared her throat, "of quotas."

"Quotas?" Harriet screwed up her face in disgust.

"If you're not done by the end of the day then you'll be obliged to stay on. We're almost there but we have to band together, push on."

"Quotas…?" Harriet repeated, her outrage growing by the second.

"And I don't expect to hear any complaints about it—particularly in light of our wonderful night at the Palomar."

"Not to mention *after* the Palomar," Clara smirked.

"And there's half a dozen tickets to the Premiere up for grabs for girls who excel."

"The Premiere—?" Maggie pricked up her ears.

"Red carpet and all," Clara said, "Milt already said I'm going."

"Any questions?" Mary straightened papers on her desk and flicked her skirt again.

"But that's not fair, what do we get out of it?" Harriet hissed.

The room filled with whispering as the unwelcome news sunk in. "Back to work," Mary ordered, approaching Maggie's desk. "Maggie, we'll start you on lines today."

"Really?" Maggie turned to Harriet, "Hattie—I'm on lines, how do you like that?"

"Terrific," Harriet drawled, "good for you."

When Mary stepped out for a dose of nicotine the room filled with low, urgent murmurs. "Miss grumpy's gonna flip her wig," Clara said, indicating Harriet with a nod.

"Damned right I am," Harriet fumed, "we bust our guts and what thanks do we get?"

"Plenty," Clara countered, "Palomar cost him an arm and a leg y'know."

"Yeah well maybe he oughta sell the other arm and leg and hand over the profits." Harriet scooted her chair over to convene with Dora and the two began talking in low, angry tones.

"I guess it's not so bad," Maggie said, lured as she was by the thought of winning a gold ticket to the premiere of *The Little Orphan,* especially if it meant arriving on Art's somewhat bony arm. She turned to Clara as the tip of her brush dipped into black paint. "We ought to work quickly after all," she decided, "get the job done."

"Sure." Clara leaned back and yawned, "whats you put in is whats you get out."

"And it's only a *little* sacrifice," Maggie muttered, suddenly aware of the ache in her wrist.

"They're troublemakers," Clara thumbed over her shoulder at the dissenters.

"And we're all very lucky to have jobs at all," Maggie said, doing her best to ignore the heated conversation taking place behind her, the growing congregation at Dora's desk.

"Don't bother me one way or the other." Clara smiled secretively and fingered a glittering bracelet. Maggie's eyes bugged.

"Diamonds?"

"Yep. The real McCoy—we're going steady."

"You and Milton?"

"Hey—" Clara scowled, "don't act so surprised, we're in love, see?"

"Of course, yes…"

"We *are*," Clara insisted, regarding Maggie petulantly, "oh don't act so high and mighty—we spent the whole night together, so what?" She twirled the bracelet and her eyes filled with moon. "Didn't ask for it neither."

"It's beautiful," Maggie said, tuning in to the distraction behind her.

"We deserve a pay rise," Harriet was saying, "time we did something about it—whaddya say?"

"Hear hear!"

"Seven years," came another voice, "surely that oughta count for something."

Maggie rested her brush on the little metal tray and spoke in a low voice, "I suppose it would help lift morale, a pay rise."

"I'll be outta here before you can say boo to a cow," Clara shrugged carelessly and Maggie's brow furrowed.

"Oh but you're not leaving are you? You can't—our Orphan needs all the help she can get—you're one of our steadiest hands, it'd be a waste."

"Yeah and that ain't all they're good for neither." Clara twitched her eyebrows and Maggie, repelled by the straight-talk, shook out her wrist and returned to work. It was all very well for Clara to follow her instincts, but need she discuss them so flagrantly? "Aw relax will ya? Miss hoity-toity. Thought you was on safari anyways?"

"Well," Maggie began, reluctant to reveal more to Harley Studio's resident chatter-box. Her feelings for Art were much safer tucked away without too much airing.

"By the looks of it you got your hooks in a couple of fish," Clara nodded knowingly.

"You don't fish on safaris," Maggie pointed out.

"Huh?" Clara's pretty nose crinkled.

"You hunt. Not fish."

"What?"

"Safaris. Giraffes and elephants and lions and so on. Not fish. I believe you've mixed your metaphor or some such thing." She frowned, unsure if Clara had used any kind of metaphor in the first place.

"Metaphor huh? Well I ain't got time for that kind of malarkey. Point is, I see what I see. Capeesh?"

"No, I don't capeesh at all."

"Seems to me I ain't the only one round here fishing for a guy with deep pockets."

"What on earth can you mean?"

"*Oh Mr Harley*—" Clara mugged, affecting a fair version of Maggie's upper-crust accent, "I couldn't possibly accept a lift in your *off*-al fancy car." She fluttered her lashes and made a bow of her lips.

"Mr Harley?" Maggie said, her confusion growing.

"Yup, you and me both shacked up with bigwigs—like the sound of that?" She raised a pencil-thin brow, arranged her face primly and let out a throaty laugh, "all official mind you—nothin' shady."

"What the heck are you about?" Maggie said, scrambling to understand.

"Not a patch on Milt," Clara went on, twisting the diamond-clad bracelet wistfully, "yeah I can see it now, you and me living the high life in Bel-Air mansions."

"What *are* you about?" Maggie demanded.

"Don't act all innocent, Milt says he's gone ga-ga," she snorted, "watching you like a hawk while you was dancing with the ugly fella."

"Ugly? Why Art's nothing of the sort—"

"Ask me old chrome-dome's the safe bet…nah, forget the union fella."

"Quiet!" It was Mary, returned from her self-imposed fumiga-tion. The chattering stopped and the door, letting out a painful, somewhat comical squeak, closed behind their leader.

"Yup," Clara continued in a whisper, "he sure got it bad, snooping round to get another look at you—I say grab him while you can."

"What? You don't mean *Ted* do you? The fix-it man?"

"Fix it man?" Clara squinted in disbelief, "he's Milt's brother, dummy."

"Ted?"

"Ted, Edward—ask me the guy's a wet fish, and I'm not mixing no metaphors on that account—"

"*Quiet*, ladies." Mary replaced the telephone in the cradle and put down her pen, "good news—seems quite a few of you got lucky this week." She regarded her charges unsmilingly and read out the list of women invited to see the latest rushes, a weekly privilege bestowed on a select few. "…Clara Selden, Patricia Isenberg, Mary Alameda, Amelia Andrews—" and last but not least, Maggie Goodwin.

"What I tell ya?'" Clara turned to Maggie and winked, "you and me kid, on easy street."

Maggie left for lunch, picking up the pace to shake Clara from her tail. She took a left instead of a right then headed to the nearest exit. Whether she'd snagged Edward or Ted via hook or gun she was in no mood to discuss the matter, and convincing Clara the so-called capture had been accidental was utterly useless. Maggie's account of the situation had fallen on deaf ears —she wasn't the least interested in fish with little to no facility to carry on a decent conversation—even if that fish did have an *off*-al fancy car and rather stellar connections.

She escaped into a narrow service alley, weaving through a maze of trash cans with her sketch-pad clamped under her arm. "Oh hallo," she said, suddenly in the company of two men squatting on upturned crates. "Mmm—smells marvelous," she enthused, motioning to the half-open door behind them, "kitchen? Food? You eat?…Wonderful," she added, the men bursting into laughter as she scurried away.

She took refuge in the shade of a eucalyptus tree, resting against the trunk among shards of shedded bark, and after stuffing down four stale ginger-nut cookies she set about business, still mad with Clara and her unwarranted assertions.

Maggie Goodwin, independent pant-wearing woman on a mission would get ahead through sweat and tears alone, not via diamond bracelets or sidling up to a Harley brother. "Easy street?" she muttered angrily—it was simply pot-luck she'd been invited to see the rushes, nothing more than chance.

She smiled at the thought of seeing Art again. They might

very well sit together and discuss the Orphan's progress…not to mention their promised supper date. She watched a beetle crawl into a bark tube then opened her sketchpad, determined to get the thing done. If she worked non-stop her squirrel's inaugural adventure might be roughed out by then. She would get Art's go-ahead to employ his raccoon, and if Milton happened to have a spare moment or two she might wave the thing under his nose as well.

"Hey you—"

Maggie came to with a jolt, a stubby, midday shadow falling across her face. "Don't sweat it," Harriet said, "we got a few minutes yet." A gust of wind lifted a sheet into the air and Harriet, perpetually primed to fight or take flight, lunged instinctively to catch the wayward sketch. "How's she coming along, your wannabe?"

"She's very cleverly learned to surf."

"Say…she's terrific, real terrific."

"Thank you. Yes I rather thinks she is."

"Come along then."

Harriet pulled Maggie to her feet and they made their way back to Paint and Ink, both of them silent and dreading the afternoon slog. "Better get a move-on or you'll lose your privileges."

"Privileges?" Maggie balked.

"The viewing room." Harriet stole a look at Maggie as they took the short-cut around the administration building, the rebellious trail worn in the grass from countless hurrying feet.

"Oh that, yes—terrific luck getting pulled out of the hat."

"Hat? Huh. Guess you wanna get close to the action?" Harriet raised her eyebrows.

"That's right, give my squirrel the best shot."

"You know it's funny," Harriet began, intoning her prelude with care, "I never got pulled out of that hat."

"Never?" Maggie caught her cheek between her teeth, "why that's too bad."

"Nope—not a once. And that's a fact."

Maggie swallowed hard, cringing inwardly, her thoughts in an unpleasant jumble. Clara, she suddenly recalled, had been pulled out of the hat twice lately, and both times in the last month. Of course there was room for serendipity in any equation, but at some point math had to take over.

"You know why I never got pulled out of that hat? Cause there ain't no hat, and whats you put in ain't always whats you get out." Maggie fixed her eyes on Building C as Harriet's words hung in the air.

"Listen—I had no idea Ted was a Harley."

"No?" Harriet said as they arrived at Paint and Ink.

"No."

They regarded each other warily before Harriet spoke again. "Listen, couple of us are meeting for coffee tomorrow night."

"Oh?" Maggie stalled, "you and Dora?"

"Uh-huh, she'll be there. Care to join us?"

Maggie's heart warmed. The thought of spending an evening with real-life humans instead of imaginary beasts was terribly appealing. Even if they did have different ideas about quotas and hats she figured they could all still be friends. "Yes," Maggie said as they arrived at Room 27C with less than a minute to spare, "I'd be glad to come along, very glad indeed."

Chapter Seven

The neon sign jutted from the flat-roofed diner like a sore thumb. Behind it, a rather frightening cross-eyed clown supped on a giant striped straw. And after consulting her compact Maggie felt satisfied, pleased she'd taken more time than usual to apply powder and neaten her brows. She wouldn't go so far as to remove them entirely and draw them back on like Clara did, *that* was a pluck or two too far. She checked her teeth, tucked a misbehaving curl under her hat and slipped the compact in her purse.

Harriet hadn't arrived yet. As far as she could make out. She scanned the long row of identical booths along the windowed-wall as she sat at the counter, swiveling her stool and ogling the glass domes and their captive treats. Pecan-pie, brownies, donuts and all manner of cookies and cakes, all set off most favorably by the bracing smell of coffee.

As the waitress filled Maggie's mug the door opened and in came Harriet, Dora, and a woman Maggie didn't recognize, a dark-haired beauty in a floral dress…linked arm in arm with none other than Art. Maggie, consumed by a strange mix of horror and delight, pasted a hasty smile on her twitching face.

"There you are," Harriet said in her usual flat drawl, as though life were something to endure rather than enjoy.

"Hallo stranger," came Art's cheery greeting. "Maggie, this here is Adelita."

"How do you do?" Maggie shook hands with the startling woman before shifting her attention back to Art. "I've been waiting for you to telephone," she began unwisely, "but didn't supply you with a number."

"Didn't you?" Art said playfully, "well that's mighty odd." Maggie flashed him a smile before stealing another look at his companion, the curly hair pinned away from large dark eyes and round, striking face.

"We women can't expect you men to do all the work now can we?"

"A lady of independent spirit," Art said.

"That's right, no good fading into the background, won't get far with that kind of thinking."

"Sure, I'll keep it in mind," Art grinned.

"Huntington Park. Maggie Goodwin—look me up."

"Got it." He winked, a simple action setting off a tremendous effect, a reddened cheek and thumping of heart. She felt the beat in her chest, a bit like a conga or bongo drum, uneven and unexpected but pleasurable all the same.

"Available most nights," she added, "between my sketching and ruining my eyesight—oh and I've news about your raccoon, delightful news—"

"Raccoon?" Adelita, evidently annoyed, shot Art a sharp look.

"It's nothing, forget it," he waved his hand dismissively, "I'll fill you in you later."

"Where we sit?" Adelita drew him close, "same place?"

"Good a place as any," Art agreed.

As Adelita led the way to a booth at the rear of the diner, Maggie gulped. *Later…?* "The pies look delicious," she said, rallying her spirits as they squeezed into the booth.

"Pecan is very good. Very recommend," Adelita said.

"Well then," Maggie motioned to the waitress, "coffee and pecan-pie all round please."

"Just coffee for me," Harriet said hurriedly.

"What? Don't say you've lost your appetite?" Maggie cried, addressing the rest of the group, "Hattie's an absolute wolf at lunch. Gobbles the lot then goes in for seconds most days—let's see that appetite in action, my treat."

"Well okay," Harriet relented.

"We mustn't cheat ourselves—*and that's an order girls*—we *must* have pie."

As they devoured the sweet, nutty confection Maggie kept an eye on Adelita, leaning into Art's shoulder as though it were the most natural thing in the world, and with every private glance, word and touch the reality became clearer, the imposing woman with the impressive bust just had to be his sweetheart.

"Now what's this about my raccoon?" He regarded Maggie mildly.

"He's had a marvelous adventure, and all behind Uncle Milt's back." Her eyes sparkled with mischief.

"Oh? How so?"

"You won't be angry he ran off for a time. You see I've put him in with my squirrel. On a leaf-boat—I found the dearest little stream in Griffith Park."

"You took the liberty of stealing my raccoon for the day?"

"Guilty as charged," Maggie quipped, "but squirrel needed a companion to talk things over, after the battle you see, so all of a sudden—" she clicked her fingers for effect— "hey presto there he was—darling as ever and dressed as a butler…serving drinks as a matter of fact—he starts *out* as a cloud, then leaps out of the sky to help out, and…" she trailed off, aware of Adelita's expression, the foreboding frown and eyes like flint.

"What this raccoon?" she demanded.

"Oh, just another critter stuck under Milt's boot," Art said, grinding his cigarette into the tray for effect.

"Boot?"

"You see he's a cartoon raccoon," Maggie let out a nervous giggle, "and he won't be under Milt's boot much longer, not if I have anything to do with it."

"And how do you figure that?" Art said, fidgeting and twisting his mug on the table.

"I got my ways," she said, eyeing him flirtatiously, "don't you see? When Uncle Milt—when Mr Harley sees how our critters fit together he won't have the heart to say no—"

"Heart?" Dora scoffed.

"*Who* fit together?" Adelita fumed.

"Forget it," Art said.

"Forget it? Why I should say not. Your raccoon *will* see the light of day, he simply must." Maggie landed her fist on the table and her plate clattered under the impact.

"Don't you think we got bigger problems than stupid raccoons and squirrels?" Dora muttered under her breath.

"Ah, what's the point anyways." Art stared at the table as he snatched Adelita's pie-crust from under her nose. She glared at him fondly.

"But you'll take a look at her won't you?" Maggie said, much deflated, "at my squirrel…?"

"Chances are there's a gun in that bag so guess the answer is yes."

"Gun?" Adelita said, now even more annoyed, "what this talk?"

"Are you part of the Harley family too Adelita?" Maggie enquired, eager to ease the tension.

"Works down at Dolmans," Art said as though Maggie ought know the place.

"Make the cloze," Adelita explained.

"Close?" Maggie squinted, struggling to comprehend.

"*Close,*" Adelita said, irritated by Maggie's stupidity, "you know the shirt and pant—big place down river." Adelita dug into her crustless pie roughly.

"*Dolmans.*" Art lit another cigarette, "don't know it?"

"Sounds familiar, but no I don't believe I do, ought I?"

"You no read paper?" Adelita thumbed at Maggie, "head in sand."

"Well you see I don't have much time for papers—"

"Too busy with her squirrel," Dora chimed in, "and the goddamned Orphan."

"I fill you in," Adelita fixed her gaze on the tall woman with the long neck and lively eyes, "we on strike now three weeks."

"Oh—I *do* know Dolmans come to think of it," Maggie said, pleased with herself, "down by the river, yes—do you enjoy it? Making clothes?" Adelita crossed her arms and regarded Maggie with contempt.

"No."

"Oh…but it's terribly useful, I think."

"We get what we want, *then* I like. Maybe."

"Uh-huh, that's fair." Harriet rotated her plate and attacked her pie from the rear.

"We could learn a few things from you Dolman gals," Art said with something approaching admiration, and, as Adelita kissed her fingertips and pressed them to his cheek, Maggie spluttered, a crumb lodging in her throat. She held a napkin to her mouth, coughing and struggling to regain her composure.

"Pardon me," she managed finally, her face red from effort.

"Wrong pipe?" Art asked, giving her back a firm slap.

"I guess," Maggie blinked away tears. "Ah. That's better." She returned to her pie and dissected a more delicate portion. "Are your conditions so very bad?" Adelita folded her arms and leaned back.

"We want raise, four dollar a week—and close shop."

"You want to close the place down? Why on earth would you

want that?" Maggie asked, appealing to the group, "you won't have a job then."

"No, no, no. *Is* close shop. You no in union—you no work in factory."

"*Closed* shop," Harriet clarified.

"Oh!" Maggie laughed, "I see my mistake, yes, *closed* shop, got it."

"You think this funny business?" Adelita glared.

"Why no," Maggie backtracked, "of course not."

"The boss run scared like baby back to mama."

"Atta girl," Art said as though geeing on a winner at the track.

"It's a great shame," Maggie sighed gravely, "I only wish there were more fair men in the world—there oughta be a law about it."

"Fair huh? Like Mr Harley you mean?" Dora fiddled with her napkin as Maggie poured more sugar in her coffee, the spoon clanging conspicuously in the mug.

"It's only…well, we should be grateful for what we've got, that's what I think." She looked up, aware of the sudden silence as she turned to Dora uneasily. "Have I said something wrong…? The quotas aren't *so* bad are they? Besides, we ought to work fast," she drew in a deep breath, determined to stick to her opinion—she was entitled to it, just as others were entitled to theirs. "And I won't let Independent beat us."

"*Won't let Independent beat us,*" Dora mocked, shaking her head in dismay, "spoken like a true Harley convert. Geez she sure fell for it—hook line and sinker."

"But the quotas won't be forever—"

"Oh yeah?" Harriet stared at the table, "says who? Give Milt an inch and he'll take a mile."

"But don't you want to be part of it all? Making history?"

"History…Pah!" Dora scoffed.

"And if we give it our all there's tickets to the Premiere," Maggie said, turning to Adelita to explain.

"For *some* of us," Harriet pointed out.

"Those of us willing to knuckle down to hard work."

"Listen to Miss goody-two-shoes will ya?" Dora sneered.

Maggie, evading the gaze of friends who'd suddenly become opponents, sniffed. She licked the last of her pie from the spoon, feeling more than a little sheepish….it was true, she *had* sounded rather too much like their common enemy, the dreaded Sergeant Mary.

"This one opens her mouth without thinking," Art said.

"What bunk. I was taught to speak my mind…speak my mind and do what's best."

"What's best huh?" Dora sucked her teeth, "kind of depends what side of the fence you're on don't it?"

"Not one miserable pay rise in all these years," Harriet muttered.

"We all muddle along," came Maggie's thoughtless comment.

"Guess she's still got them rose-glasses on," Harriet said, "didn't we all?"

"Blinded by the great man," Dora drawled.

"He is a great man," Maggie said, stubbornness setting in, "a little grumpy from time to time but we ought to support him, at least for the time being."

"Oh yeah?" Dora said, "and why do you suppose that is?"

"We're in this together aren't we? A family, of sorts…" Maggie eyed the constellation of crumbs on her plate, suddenly longing for home, for cheery breakfasts of eggs over-easy, cranberry juice and generous bouts of lively conversation. "I'm glad to have a job at all."

"Yeah—bet Milt's real glad about his Bel Air mansion," Dora snorted.

"Don't forget Beverly Hills," Harriet added.

"But if we stir up trouble now—"

"Oh so we're troublemakers are we?" Dora's voice rose in anger.

"I didn't mean that," Maggie said, scrambling to explain her meaning, "I just think it's best we band together for the time being, don't you want to make history? I know I do."

"History, *shmistory*. Sure, Milt's always making history—every morning when he eats his Wheaties. Quick! Call the *Hollywood Reporter* it's a scoop!"

"Listen," Maggie said, her patience wearing thin, "I'm only saying why draw battle-lines, take sides like children squabbling over toys?"

"Oh we ain't talking toys. Nu-uh," Dora said, her eyes glinting dangerously.

"Say—go easy on her," Art said, coming to the defense of their wet-eared colleague. Maggie, ignoring Adelita's laser-like gaze, shot him a grateful look.

"Surely there's enough trouble in the world already," Maggie reasoned. She drained the last of her coffee as weighty thoughts descended on their little group. Proclamations of imminent invasions and the inevitable war looming in Europe, the black cloud threatening to block out the sun once again. It didn't bear thinking about.

"Who's for bowling?" Art said, breaking the spell of melancholy.

"Yes! Yes!" Adelita clapped, "but I beat *you*." She poked a finger at Art's chest and he turned to the others.

"You gals in?"

"Not a chance," Dora shuddered, "not after last time."

"Fell flat on her keister." Art whistled from the corner of his mouth and rolled his eyes as Adelita squeezed from the booth and headed to the restroom.

"Gotta get back to Walt," Harriet said gloomily.

"How's he doing?" Art asked, regarding her with concern.

"Oh you know Walt—still kicking."

"You gonna beat me too?" Art turned to Maggie.

"Well you see I never bowled before—"

"All the more reason to give it a shot wouldn't you say? Hard work reaps rewards and all that."

"No, thank you all the same…think I'll run along."

She gathered her belongings, suddenly exhausted from weeks of burning the candle at both ends, painting all day and sketching all night. The day before she'd even nodded off at her desk, a three-second nap that had ended in a ruinous black smudge *and* an extra hour of daily incarceration.

"But you'll telephone won't you?" Maggie said before Adelita had a chance to return.

"That supper I owe you," Art nodded, "you got it."

"We'll hatch a plan." Her expectant look was met with a frown, "my squirrel and your raccoon…their adventure together."

"Sure," he grinned then turned to Harriet, "say hi to Walt for me."

"Uh-huh. I'll try get him down Morley Hall."

"Drag him if you have to. You tell him we need him."

"We go?" Adelita, returned from the restroom, rested her hand on Art's shoulder as she adjusted her shoe.

"We go," Art affirmed, "vamos."

"Va–*ma*–nos." Adelita slapped him playfully, "you dope."

"See? Gets *that* right every time," he laughed.

As they made their way out of the cosy diner, Art, following close on Maggie's tail, rested a hand at the small of her back and she felt a sudden flip-flopping within—a strange disruption that couldn't be blamed on pie.

"Are they sweethearts?" Maggie asked as she and Harriet parted ways with the rest of the group.

"On and off."

"For how long?" Maggie wondered, rubbing her aching wrist.

"Couple of years I guess. Say, how's that wrist holding up?"

"Sore."

"Uh-huh. Me too." Harriet let out a gigantic yawn.

"But will they marry do you suppose?"

"Who knows. Not engaged, far as I know."

Maggie bit the inside of her cheek, frowning at an ill-kempt child rummaging through trash on the sidewalk, "well I think there's something terribly interesting about him…and he looks like James Cagney don't you think? I do…"

Chapter Eight

"This way, dummy." Clara dragged Maggie in the opposite direction. The viewing room was in the basement of Building A, not on the first floor as Maggie had thought. "Ain't it adorable?" Clara thrust out her chest for examination. Since the night of the Palomar her collection of jewels had expanded to include a magnificent brooch set with deep-green emeralds, "guess green's not so bad after all."

"Holy Moly!" Maggie exclaimed, suitably impressed as they hurried along the corridor, "Mr Harley'll be there won't he?"

"He's the boss ain't he?" Clara slid her hand over the railing as they took the stairs to the basement, "why the hell else would I go?"

"To see things in action, see how our Orphan's shaping up… perhaps be of some *use*."

"Use? What the hell you talking about?"

"He'll want to know what we think won't he?"

"Nope." Clara shook her head and patted a lock of tortured hair, "want my advice?"

"Not particularly."

"Just look pretty and keep your kisser shut. Take it from me, you don't wanna rock no boat."

"I'll do no such thing," Maggie declared ambiguously, striding faster to take the lead.

Her skin rose in a rash of goosebumps as she sat in the back row of the overly-cool theatre. "Thanks," she whispered, gratefully accepting Clara's coat.

"Milt's got an eye on a mink," she said, leaning in to shove Maggie with her shoulder.

"Has he? Wonderful…"

Distracted, Maggie scanned the front rows of the little theatre and identified Art's slightly large head among Milt's top men. A smiled curved her lips. She was now in the very room Wild Willie and Marley Moose had begun their lives, beloved characters who'd ventured beyond the screen to material incarnations—the countless Willie and Marley-themed toys, posters and watches gracing the shelves at local drugstores.

Milton, a shadowy figure in the dim light, signaled to the projectionist. "Quiet please," he ordered before taking a seat with his men, and as the humble film-strip clacked through the projector, the drawings sprang to life…

The Orphan, waking at daybreak and watched over by a gang of protective forest critters, a tiny bird buzzing and tugging at a golden lock with its stubby beak, the coil stretching then springing back to frame the Orphan's sleepy face…

"How on earth do they manage it?" Maggie hissed, suddenly wondering if she'd ever be capable of creating such life-like motion.

"Shh—" Clara warned.

"Stop." Milton raised his hand and the film froze, "that bird yours John?" He turned to one of the silhouette heads.

"Sure is," John confirmed.

"That'll work," Milton nodded, "much better."

"It's wonderful," Maggie called out from the back stalls, heads turning as the film rolled on. She waved to Art but he turned back to the screen just as his raccoon leapt to the Orphan's shoulder. "There he is," Maggie whispered, feeling Clara's stiff mop against her cheek, "isn't he adorable?"

"*Who's* adorable?" Clara teased as the raccoon tickled the Orphan's nose with a furious trill of whiskers.

"Stop." Milton flicked his hand and the critter froze mid-bound. "Roll back will you? The dammed thing's a mess." He raked his hand through his hair as the film played over, the raccoon bounding onto the Orphan's shoulder once more. "Stop!" He jumped up, jabbing a furious finger at the screen, "what the hell's up with its legs? Dammed thing's arthritic." There was silence, none of the men willing to air an opinion on the alleged rusty joints.

"He is a *little* stiff," Maggie offered truthfully from out of the dark. Art's raccoon may have been as cute as a bug's ear but the leap from forest floor to shoulder was far less impressive than the bird's uncanny landing on the Orphan's golden locks. "Just a little stiff…in my opinion." The men turned to face the interloper who dared speak her mind.

"Who's that?" Milton, his face lit by a shaft of light like an-expressionist monster, peered into the dark.

"It's Maggie," she waved, half-stood, then sat, "I see what you mean about the arthritis…he isn't an elderly raccoon is he Art?— Mr Schrieber?"

"Nope," Art confirmed, "matter of fact he's in the prime of his life."

"You better fix this," Milton warned his under-performer, "you're slipping, too many distractions."

"Wiseguy," Clara hissed under her breath.

"Fact of the matter is," Art said in a firm, level voice, "you get rushed along, you're gonna get a little stiff."

There was silence, then a standoff, Milton's form suddenly resembling a viper about to strike. "I won't have you talking to me that way!" he exploded, "we got a job to do and all I ask is you damned-well do it!" His chest heaved, and after a brief but violent coughing fit he continued, "that clear everyone? Now roll it will you—"

Maggie shrank in her seat as the projector resumed its clacking…never in her life had she heard such yelling coming from a grown man. Her father's repertoire consisted of diplomatic argument followed by the occasional stern word, however, to Maggie's great relief, the tense mood was soon settled by more perfection from John's little bird, and by the time the rushes were over, Milton's wits had seemingly returned.

"It's only the first bit where his knees are stiff," Maggie whispered as she shuffled into the aisle on the heel of the quick-footed Clara, "for the most part his joints seem to work rather well," she insisted, hurrying to the door to catch Art before he got too far away.

"Not so fast," Clara said, tugging Maggie back into the room just as Art disappeared at the end of the passageway.

"Any you girls interested in taking a little tour?" Milton asked.

"Boy…would I ever," Maggie exclaimed.

"Oh yes please," said another Paint and Inker, Amelia.

"Ed will take you round," Milton said as his brother appeared from out of the shadows. "Camera-room?"

"Sure," Ted said.

"You've been here all along?" Maggie said, feeling a little awkward, "I didn't recognize you, as a silhouette—but I guess I ought to—you do stand out." She cleared her throat, "being tall and all is what I'm getting at…" He regarded her quizzically, his eyes lively, curious. Maggie laughed, "matter of fact you all look like shadow puppets from the back row," she explained, turning to the boss, "reminds me of *The Adventures of Prince Ahmed* but not quite as menacing, do you know it? We organized a screening in our film group back East."

"I know it," Milton said in a pleasant enough tone.

"Lotte Reiniger—a pioneer in the field I believe, the first to move backgrounds around—like our fancy new camera will do for us—what's it called again?"

"Multi-plane camera," Ted said helpfully.

"That's right, figured it out all on her own. Smart lady." She eyed Milton hopefully, and with the memory of his tantrum all but forgotten, grabbed at the chance to present her sketchpad. "Now Mr Harley while I have your attention, won't you please take another look at my squirrel? I think you'll find her very much matured." She opened the cover and waited, ready to turn the page at his pleasure, but there was no pleasure at all. Instead, he pushed the book away and regarded her as if she were a fly he'd like to swat.

"What in god's name is the matter with you people?" he muttered, turning to his brother, "take her away will you?"

Maggie's cheeks flamed. Her blood boiled, her jaw clenching as she followed blindly at the rear of the small group, her head bowed to conceal her mounting fury. She barely remembered leaving one room and arriving at another so great was her indignation, her urge to turn back and demand the tiny slice of attention she'd been denied.

As Ted ushered the women into the camera-room he nodded, but as Maggie passed the threshold he spoke. "Sorry bout that. Gets a little worked up…you could say."

"Evidently," Maggie snapped, still smarting from the unpleasantness of it all, "I only hope he doesn't treat you like that."

"Well, from time to time—guess I'm kind of used to it. "

"Pity. One should never get used to rudeness." Ted glanced over at the other women, watching their tete-a-tete with quite a deal of interest.

"He's not so bad, once you figure out how to handle him."

"With a thick pair of gloves I'd suggest."

"Just a bear with a sore head is all, got a ton on his mind."

"Bear?" Maggie frowned, softening at the fondness in his voice, "more like...well now let's see...more like a hyena I'd say."

"You might be on to something there," Ted said, rubbing his bald pate thoughtfully.

"A perfect fit I should think," she said, picturing Milton as a chain-smoking, tantrum-throwing scavenger. "Uh huh, hyena is just the thing," she decided, all at once noting the reason for Ted's startling eyes...his lashes must have been the thickest and darkest she'd ever seen without the aid of artifice, and rather astonishing for someone with...well...no hair. He grinned and the resemblance to his brother became suddenly apparent. "Why didn't you say you were brothers?"

"Didn't know huh?" He glanced at the other Paint and Inkers again, conscious of their chuckling.

"Well you might have said," Maggie sighed, "here I was thinking you were a fix-it man."

"Would it be so bad if I was?"

"Well...no, but why didn't you say?"

"Uh..." he trailed off, clearly run out of steam. "Bill—" he gestured to the man operating an odd-looking machine, one of the cameras Maggie supposed, "show the ladies the ropes would you?"

"Sure thing," Bill hoisted his leg over the bench, stretched his arms and shook the stiffness from his knees, "step this way ladies, let me introduce you to my *best* friend."

"Well, so long," Maggie said, eager to join her colleagues.

"Say—" Ted touched her arm lightly, "you get yourself a set of wheels yet?"

"No time. What with my squirrel...and staying on top of the quotas."

"How bout I look out for you, make sure you don't get hoodwinked this time?"

"Okay...sure—if you like," she glanced over her shoulder

impatiently, annoyed to find the demonstration had begun without her.

"Then this little sucker flips over the top, see?" Bill said as he placed the cell onto the guide-pegs and closed the glass plate on top.

"Hey, I did that—" Amelia said, pointing proudly to Prince green-pants. Maggie squeezed between bodies to get a better look as Bill pressed a lever with his foot. There was a flash of light and a satisfying loud click.

"There—one frame closer to the end."

"The end? *Yes* please," Amelia laughed as Bill removed the cell now committed to film.

"And then—" he took the next cell and placed it under the glass.

"Lemmie guess," Maggie chimed in, "you do it all over?"

"Yup. Got it in one."

Poised with pencil and paper, Maggie took notes as Bill worked up to speed, replacing each of the painted cells with the next, then the next, then the next, his arms and legs moving as though part of the machine itself. "Easy as that," Maggie muttered as a plan took shape in her mind, a plan that would surely lead to the capture of Milton Harley's full attention—and no gun required.

Later that evening, Maggie settled in her usual chair and cast an eye over the growing collection of papers and pencils surrounding her like a fort. She frowned, squinting at the page in the dusky light, still angry at Milton, "I'll show you…Mr Hyena." She dunked her cookie in a glass of milk, munched greedily and dusted off her hands, glancing at the telephone, willing it to ring.

Perhaps he *had* phoned while she was out at the drugstore, or stuck in traffic on the trolley-car…or was Art busy getting cosy with Adelita somewhere? They might be patching things up, bowling perhaps or doing god-knows what god-knew where?

Her hand swept across the page as she plotted the position of the furry sweethearts drifting over the horizon on the sea-worthy leaf. "That's it! Lilly! *Squirrel Lilly*—how do you like that?" A smile engulfed her face as she finessed the tail of her newly-christened critter, "he'll see we're no pushovers..."

Her plan would take a bit of doing, but Milton's dismissal had set her determination like stone. Somehow she'd get access to the camera-room and get her squirrel on film. Milton was far more likely to pay attention if Lilly was leaping and cavorting right in front of his face. She frowned at the page, somewhat daunted by the steps ahead—concocting a cunning plan was one thing, but carrying it out was quite another.

The telephone rang out and she leapt from the chair as if her life depended on it. "Hallo—?" Maggie's heart pounded. She gripped the receiver tight.

"Maggie?" came the male voice.

"The one and only," she sang in her usual way, confused for an instant, "Art...?" The voice was deeper than the one she'd hoped to hear.

"It's Ted. Ted Harley."

"Oh, Ted," she fiddled with the cord and quashed her disappointment, "you got my number..."

"I looked you up."

"Of course, yes, how silly of me."

"Think I found you a car."

"Have you?" Maggie said, suddenly feeling bad.

"Uh-huh. Ford roadster, in mighty-fine condition too. Think you oughta take a look."

"A roadster huh? Sounds awful sporty...is she?"

"I'll drive her round and you can see for yourself."

"Tonight?" Maggie balked, "gee, it's a little late—"

"Not now," he laughed, "how about Friday. Pick you up bright and early, you can see how she feels."

"Oh there's no need to—"

"Seven okay?"

"Why yes of course," Maggie said, shaking off the last of her bad feelings, "it's very kind of you."

"No trouble at all." An awkward silence ensued.

"Well then, good night Ted."

She placed the receiver in the cradle and scowled at the mirror above the telephone-table. Evidently Clara had been right about Edward Harley. He had taken a shine to her. But he certainly hadn't gone ga-ga *or* bananas. On the contrary, Ted seemed a steady type, a man of few words who got things done, not a man liable to grand romantic gestures. "A practical man," Maggie told herself, setting her mind at ease.

She switched on the bathroom light and set about brushing her teeth, vowing to tread a very careful line, make sure the situation between them remained strictly platonic…besides, she reasoned, if Ted ever looked to be entering a dangerous state of swoon, she need only apply the brakes and set him straight on the matter. To avoid disappointment on his part.

Chapter Nine

*M*aggie waved as Ted smiled up at her from behind the wheel of a superbly shiny dark-blue beauty. "Be right with you," she yelled, gathering her belongings and flying down the stairs two at a time, only slowing to avoid the perils of the prickly courtyard.

The iron gate swung open and she let out an appreciative whistle, rounded the impressive machine and stood by the driver's door. "Good heavens she's *magnificent*—why and I bet she runs just as smooth as milk—no not milk—that doesn't sound right at all… what does she run like?" Ted frowned thoughtfully before replying.

"Like a well-oiled machine."

"Swell. A well-oiled machine." She should have known Ted wouldn't go in for similes or metaphors or whatever literary device her teachers had tried to drum into her without much success.

"1932 roadster, they call her The Deuce."

"Just her? Or all of them?"

"All of them I guess."

"Okay," Maggie said, opening the well-oiled door, "scoot over."

"You wanna drive?" Ted frowned in surprise, "but I thought—"

"What?"

"Thought you'd take a turn later, on the ride home—if you like her that is."

"Of course I want to drive." Maggie smiled sweetly, remembering all the trouble he'd gone to, "but you'll show me the knobs and whatnots. I promise not to kill you."

"Alright," he nodded a little grudgingly and shifted over to allow her behind the wheel. "See you got your speed right here," he began, indicating the dials before moving on to the levers, "and this here's the horn, then you got your indicators here—then ah...oh—you got your ignition right up here on the steering column, now that's real new, real smart," he peered at her from under the rim of his trilby, "but it's tricky, you gotta be sure and toggle see, when you take the key out," he reached a lanky arm over her lap to demonstrate.

"Toggle huh? Got it."

"Yup, that way the wheel locks up and no one can take her."

"You don't say," Maggie said, genuinely impressed with the advancement, "what will they think of next?"

"Oh I don't know," he grinned, "television-machines, flying to the moon."

"Always wondered if it's made of cheese," Maggie joked as she got familiar with the brake-pedal, "but it's silly to suppose moon-people like cheese that much." She gripped the key in readiness and caught his puzzled expression, "right, let's see what she's made of—not cheese I hope."

The roadster roared to life without a hint of protest and the air filled with a healthy, even thumping, a growling, throaty purr. "Good golly—she's a lion, a great big pussycat."

"One hellava heart under that hood," he rubbed his chin thoughtfully and rested an arm over the side.

"I suppose she's got an awful lot to say and wants to shout all about it," Maggie declared, revving the engine and steering the gigantic cat into traffic.

"You? Or the pussycat?"

"Both," Maggie grinned, "and only a hundred and fifty dollars you say?"

"I could have a word if you like, try and swing a better deal?"

"Absolutely not." Maggie shifted gear and they roared past a truck. The money her father had wired was more than enough to cover it—he wouldn't hear of her scrimping again, getting lumped with another tin-can disaster. "She's worth the asking and more. Much more."

"Okay, the lady has spoken."

"She has."

"Say," Maggie said after a rather prolonged silence, "if you're not Harley's fix-it man then what are you?"

"The money man."

"Oh. An accountant?"

"Could say that, I take care of business—keep Milt on track."

"An adviser of sorts."

"Uh-huh."

"And a terrific fixer of drawers," Maggie reminded him, content to fill the journey to Burbank with small-talk, her mind quite distracted by other thoughts, namely Art's telephone call late last night, the bell ringing out just as she'd laid her head on the pillow. "Watch out!" She sounded the horn at a street peddler ranging too far from the sidewalk.

"Whoa—" Ted gripped his hat as she sped up to pass a bus spewing fumes from its rear.

"I can't get enough of this blue-sky life," Maggie said when they'd emerged from the smoke. She flashed him a smile as they cruised along, now free of the black fug, "the glorious desert."

"I guess," he rested a finger on the dashboard as they passed another stinky bus.

"You don't sound so sure."

"Same thing day in day out can get a little stale," he ventured.

"Stale, huh?" Maggie mused, "don't like the sound of that."

"Give me a few clouds now and then, know what I'm saying?"

"I know *exactly* what you mean."

She stole a glance at her passenger as they waited in traffic. He looked a little sad and she turned away, only to feel his gaze upon her, admiring her profile no doubt—the neat nose and smallish chin above long, sturdy neck. "Perhaps you oughta move out to New York, you'll get plenty of clouds out there—*and* freezing winds—*and* sweaty summers," she laughed heartily and swooped into the outside lane.

"No can do."

"No can do? Why I should think you might do as you please."

"Gotta see this thing through."

"The Orphan?"

"Uh-huh."

"Bosses orders?"

"If the Orphan tanks we might be in trouble," Ted muttered.

"But you mustn't let anything hold you back—or any*one* for that matter, no, if you want something bad enough then to hell with what other people say, just go get it."

"Go get it huh? Just like that."

"That's right. Just like that. My father drilled it into me and I'm afraid I can't change, even if I wanted to—which I don't." She let out another carefree laugh.

"You miss home?"

"Goodness no, I'm far too busy to get all sentimental."

After another good while of silent travel in which she was left to her own thoughts, or more precisely, what outfit to wear on her supper date with Art, she slowed and turned into the private road leading to the studio, relieved to find the brakes responsive. Bertha had been far less compliant in that department.

"Park next to mine," Ted pointed to a surprisingly modest-looking maroon car, and as she swung wide and maneuvered the

Deuce into the tight space he braced himself against the dash-board, "easy does it—"

"Perfect." Maggie, turning to Ted, averted her eyes as he settled his hat on his slightly-shiny egg. The engine idled in a regular, healthy thud.

"You don't do things by half do you?"

"No. Should I?"

"I guess not," Ted frowned as he mulled the thought over.

"Now let's see about this toggle thing," she turned and pressed as per Ted's instructions and swung the key to signal her success, "there, all locked up safe and sound—wait, hang on a minute, let's stay put for a bit, soak up the sun—if you can bear it."

They sat together companionably, the morning rays warming their wind-cooled skin. "How long have you worked here?"

"Coming up four years now."

"It's just with all the stories in the newspapers you'd think I'd know something of you—not that I believe everything I read, most of it's bunk—complete garbage."

"I'm not much for the limelight…all the hullaballoo."

"Not like your brother then?"

"Nope. Chalk and cheese in that regard."

"Is it difficult? But I suppose you must get along?"

"We have our moments for sure. Just a matter of know-how, getting a handle on him."

"Yes, you mentioned that," Maggie said, her grand plan coming to mind with sudden urgency, "only the sooner I figure out how to handle him the better…for the good of my squirrel if nothing else."

"Who's this Squirrel of yours?"

"Lilly, my cartoon-critter—if I'm to be an animator she needs to prove herself…thing is I got a problem, a *big* one," she dropped her voice to imitate the boss, "*we don't employ lady animators at Harley Studios Miss Goodwin.*"

"Not bad," Ted said as they stood at the entrance of Building C.

"Well the pussycat's a real beauty—*my* Pussycat."

He took a card from his pocket and shuffled nervously. "My number, in case she gives you any trouble."

"Ted—" she blurted out, her heart suddenly racing. No point beating round the bush, straight to the point worked best, "I need access to the camera-room. To get my squirrel on film." She took a piece of paper from her purse and he scanned the notes she'd taken on Bill's tour, "It's all here see? I swear to be careful—I won't break a thing, promise." His brow furrowed, not the bug-squishing, impatient look she'd suffered from his brother but a puzzled, worried look. "See? I got every step of the process, I know exactly what button does what thanks to Bill, terribly thor-ough—and Harriet says I can get film downtown…"

"Harriet Mueller?"

"Uh-huh, bit of a grump but all the same I'm rather fond of her," she tilted her head and lay her hand on his arm, "but won't you help me Ted? Please…?"

"Well I dunno…we're on a tight schedule."

"And don't I know it." She straightened, rising to her full height of five foot eleven, just a few inches shy of the younger Harley brother, "do you know how many sacrifices we've made down at Paint and Ink? Why we've even given away our morning break for the Orphan—well actually it was taken away I should say…"

Ted stiffened, his hands busy in his pockets, jingling coins or keys or whatever mysterious objects men stored in their surrogate purses. "And between you and me," she continued, swapping her strident tone for a furtive whisper, "some of the girls are getting mighty antsy about it," she nodded and made a hasty amend-ment, "*some* of us, that's to say." She glanced over his shoulder at the group of women coming towards them, Harriet and Dora among the throng.

"If Milt finds out he won't like it."

"But he won't…please?" she made her eyes round like a seal pleading for fish at a waterpark, "if only you'd arrange things so I could get in? I'll do the rest—"

"Arrange things huh?"

"Yes arrange things," Maggie brightened, sensing a ray of hope, "we'll slip in any time you like, day, night—or how about Sunday—I'm not much for church are you? Oh I know Milton won't like you going behind his back but he'll thank you in the end…"

"Well—"

"It'll be our little secret…surely you don't tell Milt *everything*, do you?"

"Nope." He straightened his shoulders and nodded as Harriet and Dora passed by, "I suppose we *could*—"

"Oh thanks a million! A million, *trillion*, million!" Maggie clasped her hands in a prayer-like gesture, her smile as bright and wide could be.

"That's a boat-load of thanks you got there."

"Uh-huh—but just the right kind of boat-load I think, just the right kind to show how grateful I am—how *terribly* grateful."

Chapter Ten

*A*fter several minutes of indecision, Maggie chose the blue smock-dress with the scalloped, white collar. In the past hour she'd downed enough coffee to wake the most weary of sleeping-beauties. She checked the time, pushed a curl behind her ear, smoothed her ever-narrowing brows and headed down to the Pussycat.

"Let's have a look-see," Maggie said, opening the glove-compartment and consulting the Thomas Guide in the dusky light. Ted had made a gift of it that morning. The guide, he'd promised, would be far more edifying than the flimsy tourist map she'd been relying on since arriving in Los Angeles. "Now look here," she'd joked, once again struck by the kindness or blueness of his eyes, "how will I survive if I don't know where Clark Gable lives?"

He was quite handsome really, if one forgot about what was under his hat, not that she understood why a man with no hair might be a lesser sort of being than any other—and how brothers could be so dissimilar in regard to follicles was a great mystery of biology, Maggie decided as she turned left at the signal and kept an eye out for the next road-sign.

Art's suggestion she expand her hamburger and ginger-nut

diet at a Mexican diner had been met with some hesitation, especially as the place was renowned for its tongue-searing salsa and red-hot tacos. She made another turn and spotted Art reading a paper at a bright-yellow outdoor table. Thoroughly alerted by the Pussycat's purr, he looked up. "Why will you look at that…"

"Meet the Pussycat…ain't she keen?" Maggie said, coming towards him and reading the festive sign above the colorful diner, "Cielito Lindo—I wonder what it means?"

"Sky something, I dunno, beats me." He folded over the *Los Angeles Times* and made room for her at the dinky table, "I took the liberty of ordering. Tacos okay?"

"Sure…I suppose Adelita would know," Maggie said, trying her best to appear casual, "what it means. Why don't you ask?"

"Good idea."

"If you see her," she added, taking stock of the condiments clustered in the centre of the table, the strange fiery sauces she had a mind to avoid. He rolled the paper in a tube, tapped it on the table and let it unfurl.

"You seen this?" He pushed it towards her, "got his stupid mug in the paper again." She rotated the paper and studied the photograph. Milton, his sleeves rolled up and foot resting proprietorially on the frame of his latest whiz-bang machine.

"…Harley breakthrough heralds new era of animation," she read out, screwing up her face. "…studio boss Milton Harley has every reason to smile in the world thanks to his brand-new multiplane camera—"

"Forty-thousand bucks apparently. He gets a new toy and we get a kick in the pants," Art said, setting in on his first taco, "little spicy?"

"A little."

"How'd you like his little tantrum the other day?"

"Not much." She opened the top of a tiny bottle of who knew what, sniffed suspiciously, and sneezed, "I'm sure he's got a lot on his mind…"

"Sure he does."

"If the Orphan tanks Harley might be in trouble and we don't want that—"

"Where'd you hear that?"

"Oh, no-place—just a silly thought." She cleared her throat and braved another bite of taco, telling herself it was much like a hamburger anyways, just meat between a cornier sort of bread.

"Well if Harley tanks I got my options."

"Oh? Bully for you mister."

In the the past month or so Maggie's options had shrunk to lining the foliage of forest tree A, lining the foliage of forest tree B, C, or even D. She pushed the paper away roughly.

"What's the matter? The Harley shine wearing off?"

"No, just figuring out how to handle Uncle Milt."

"Gotta be kidding, you got no hope…can't handle the devil—"

"Devil? Now that's a little unfair wouldn't you say? Besides, you oughta keep that kind of talk for real villains, warmongers and the like."

"Yeah but I got proof." Art grinned, slipped a pencil from his shirt-pocket and began drawing on the photograph.

"I don't see how a bad temper puts you in the same league as Mussolini or Hitler," Maggie argued as the transformation took place before her eyes. Within a minute, Milt's head had been graced with a handsome set of devilish horns. "However—" she smirked, unable to resist the temptation of getting in on the act, "if he *is* the devil then I think you missed something." She snatched the pencil away and embarked on her own embellishment, a scaly tail peeking out from under Milton's personally tailored and very expensive jacket.

"Oh *now* you're talking—" Art snatched the pencil back and disrupted Milt's million-watt smile with a set of bloody incisors. "There," he leaned back in his chair so the front legs rocked off the ground, "*now* we got the story straight."

"It's only a bit of fun," Maggie sniffed, suddenly recalling her little secret, the promised trip to the camera-room with Ted. She stretched her arms and let them drop.

"Heard Harriet's got a few more recruits down at Paint and Ink."

"I suppose she has," Maggie said, suddenly withdrawing like a clam into the sand.

"Let's take a gander at this squirrel then." He wiped his mouth, patted his stomach, and affecting a put-upon look and feigning great weariness, retrieved Maggie's sketchbook from under the table.

"Squirrel Lilly and the Giant Turtle-Wave. Her first adventure," Maggie said, "one of many I suspect."

As he examined the inaugural adventure of her rascally rodent she gulped soda in an attempt to calm her excitement, not to mention her taco-seared tongue. "Well? Don't keep me in suspense—what's the verdict?"

"Hold on a minute will you? Geez." He turned the last page, slapped the cover shut, stifled a belch and rubbed his stomach for good measure.

"Well?"

"Not bad."

"And? Do I have your say so or not?"

"For what?"

"To recruit your raccoon?"

"You already did didn't you?"

"Well yes, I suppose so."

"Aw shucks, go right ahead, he's all yours…heck—dress him up in a tutu for all I care."

"Oh—you don't like the apron, I thought you mightn't—perhaps they'll go dancing instead, crash into a few tables," she smiled encouragingly, hoping Art might get ideas about continuing their evening someplace else.

"Listen, hate to break it to you, but seems like you're having a hard time getting the message."

"What message?"

"You won't get anywhere with Uncle Milt. Believe me. He *ain't* interested."

"Won't get anywhere?" she raised her brows archly, "now that's fine talk Mr Schrieber."

"Sensible talk is what it is."

"Well I don't want to hear a bit of it, you can keep your sensible talk to yourself."

"Uh-huh. Yup, thought as much, stubborn as a mule."

"Ah but you see I got a plan with Ted—" she caught her cheek between her teeth, frowning at her mistake.

"Ted?"

"You know…Beelzebub's brother."

"Oh I get it, attacking from all fronts huh? Now that's what I call strategy," he nodded sagely, "boy you sure know what you want don't you?"

"And what if I do?"

They sat in silence as she digested the feelings churning in her gut. Finally she looked up, countering Art's grin with a steely look, "I'm only doing what any girl with spirit would."

"Oh yeah and what's that?"

"Make the best of things," she pushed a dangerous-looking red vegetable to the edge of her plate.

"Didn't think you were the type is all—but maybe you picked up a couple tips from Clara."

"Tell me," Maggie said, dodging the barb and throwing one of her own, "what's going on…with Adelita?"

"What about her?"

"Well," Maggie braved, "are you together or not?"

"Nope…used to be we had a thing going." He fiddled with the pencil and her irritation waned. "Gracias," he said to the boy taking their plates—he might have been about nine or ten Maggie guessed, either that or a malnourished twelve.

"Poor kid oughta be in school."

"He is, school of hard knocks…So, what's this plan of yours anyways? With your sweetheart, Ted."

"Ted's a friend. Just a friend."

"Friend huh? There's one for the books."

"He is," Maggie insisted, secretly pleased Art was taking notice of *her* options, "what do you make of him?"

"Not much. Stuck under Milt's boot, same as the rest of us."

"Harriet doesn't seem to think much of him…but I happen to think he's rather nice, rather kind."

"I'll fill you in on a little matter. Ed Harley gave Walter his marching orders, saw to it personally…best stay clear of him is my advice."

"I'm not sure it's the kind of advice I'm after," she eyed him coyly as he flicked his pencil on the table, "anyone might think you were jealous."

"Might be."

And just like that, Maggie's misgivings about the wavy-haired animator evaporated like hot breath from the surface of glass.

Chapter Eleven

Maggie peered through the window before stealing into the room. In her three months at Harley Studios it would be the first time she'd put a foot wrong, except for the minor infraction she refused to see as such, her failed attempt to get the attention of the boss. "Maggie——" The curt tone sliced through silence.

"I know, there's no excuse," Maggie said before Mary had a chance to embark on another hackneyed speech about punctuality. Their education on the subject had been nothing short of an indoctrination, and last week Dora's wage had been docked—reduced from a measly twenty-two dollars a week to an even more tight-fisted twenty-one. Dora's very good reason, the mad dash to the drugstore for the cough-syrup she swore by hadn't mattered a whit. Simply put, there was no place in the Harley workplace for circumstance, and it was Mary's job to beat her drum about it. Loudly.

"You know the rules. I'm obliged to report you."

"Yes Miss Donnelly, it won't happen again," Maggie said, both indignant and contrite.

She hadn't thought it possible. How could a brain switch off so thoroughly that a clanging alarm clock couldn't rouse it? She suppressed a yawn and slipped on the regulation cotton glove. In all her life she never felt so weary, and never looked so weary for that matter. There were dark circles requiring more powder than she had the patience to apply, a shocking development to behold…as indeed she had that very morning, catching her reflection in a storefront window—a dubious character, heavily shaded and slightly wild-eyed.

"It's gone too far," Harriet declared at lunch as she, Maggie and Dora took their trays outside to claim the prized table under the eucalyptus. Dora slammed down her tray and stabbed her macaroni cheese angrily.

"It's a disgrace what we're paid. The man's got a zillion dollars and he pulls the belt tighter. *Our* belts." She shook her head, disgusted at Milton's growing preference for sticks over carrots.

"Yep. Getting *real* mean." Harriet nibbled the last flesh from her apple and turned to Maggie, "least one dollar less won't send you broke."

"No," Maggie said with more prickle then she'd intended, "it won't."

"How's that plan of yours shaping up?" Harriet tossed the apple-core over her shoulder into the neatly-tended shrubbery.

"What plan? Who told you?"

"Art. Making any headway?"

"I'm working on it," Maggie said, looking away.

"What plan?" Dora asked.

"Just paving the way for us girls, right Mags? Trailblazing all the way to Building A, the first lady animator at Harley Studios."

"Fat chance," Dora snorted.

"You'll see." Maggie scooped a leaf from the ground and lay it on the table, admiring its threaded lines and bright colors. She wound it on her finger like a ring, her thoughts wandering to Art with a secret smile, the confirmed status of his bachelorhood, his jealous reaction to her friendship with Ted…

"Maggie?" Harriet leaned over the table, "hallo? Anyone home? I said *how was your date?*" Her brows danced like Groucho Marx, "good and spicy?"

"Wonderful," Maggie said. A flush rose to her cheeks.

"What?" Dora broke in, "don't say she's fallen for him too? What happened to Adelita—he throw her over again?"

"Oh you know Art, the guy can't help himself." Harriet rolled her eyes and Maggie, alarmed, unwound the leaf and pulled it taut.

"What's the big deal about him anyways?" Dora said as she polished off her macaroni. Maggie looked down, frowning at what she'd done—torn the pretty leaf in two.

"He's awful interesting, but I'm not the slightest bit dizzy on him if that's what you think. Or bananas—*or* ga-ga…I'm perfectly capable of controlling myself."

"Ask me the guy's a heel," Dora said.

"That sour-grapes talking?" Harriet laughed and promptly received a punch on the arm. Evidently there was more to the story than Dora was willing to let on.

"Art's just Art when it comes to the ladies." Harriet rubbed her shoulder where the friendly blow had landed. She bit her lip, her eyes downcast, "been a real pal to Walter, a real pal."

"What happened?" Maggie asked gently, "with Walter?"

"Same thing as half the country. Got fired."

"Yes of course I know that," Maggie said, hoping for more particulars, most notably Ted's role in the matter. They sat, silent and spent from the morning of wrist-breaking repetition, the never-ending procession of celluloid sheets marching by in the name of capital-H-history, "is he—was he an animator?"

"Nope. Gardener, you can thank him for all the pretty flowers. Knows a whole bunch about flowers," Harriet said, wistful.

"Any sign of work yet?" Dora squashed an insect intent on sharing her soda and flicked the lifeless body from her wet thumb.

"Nope. Some talk of a program down the port, but I ain't counting no chickens. Nuh-uh."

"What's the deal with Dolmans, they get what they want yet?"

"Sure did," Harriet said, perking up, "and if we play our cards right we can do the same, make some real changes round here."

Maggie, feeling the weight of two sets of expectant eyes boring into her skull, squirmed uncomfortably. "How bout you Mags? You in?"

"In…?"

"I'll put this nice and simple for ya," Dora said, "we either let Milt grind us to the bone or we do something about it?"

"But the Orphan—"

"Oh for heavens sake!" Dora glared at Maggie, exasperated, "we're not planning on shutting down the water supply—it's just a stupid film."

"It's not stupid at all," Maggie shot back, "and if the Orphan fails the whole studio might be in trouble."

"Oh yeah?" Dora seemed pleased, "says who?"

"Oh nobody," Maggie muttered.

"The only way to stick it to Milt is to pull the rug out. *Strike*."

"But surely there's other ways to make our grievances known? Better ways."

"Grievances?" Dora snorted as she thumbed at Maggie, "will you listen to this one."

"Come on then. Let's have it. What better ways?" Harriet asked.

"Negotiate. Peace talks, that kind of thing."

After all, democracy got things done. It was a lesson learned early on in Goodwin household. A Sunday's entertainment was decided by show of hands, and as the first in the air was always Maggie's little one, their cosy family of three would spend another afternoon at the picture theatre—not strolling in Central Park as Ellen Goodwin might have preferred.

"But we oughtn't resort to sabotage."

"Sabotage? Now that's just what the doctor ordered," Dora rubbed her hands, gleeful at the thought.

"But if Milton knew how we felt," Maggie insisted as Harriet's voluminous laugh rang out.

"Sure, the guy's all ears."

"What about a letter, setting out our complaints and signed by us all?" Maggie suggested, "a letter ought be the first step, much more civilized than charging in with all guns blazing."

"Been there done that," Harriet sighed, "half the girls got spooked—all we did was hand Milt a neat list of targets."

"Uh-huh, talk about backfired." Dora's body slumped in defeat.

"What if I talked to Miss Donnelly about the viewing room—"

"Viewing room?" Harriet snorted, "all I want is a fair day's pay for a fair day's work."

"And a bit of respect," Dora mumbled as she checked the time on the ever-present, ominous clock, "great, now we gotta put up with another dumb sermon."

"Least we get a break from Sergeant Mary," Harriet pointed out. She smiled weakly at Maggie.

"Uh-huh," Maggie said, rubbing her wrist and letting out a great yawn.

Come rain hail or shine all Harley employees were obliged to attend, and it wasn't long before Maggie spotted Art in the central courtyard. She figured he'd be among the stragglers ringing the outskirts of the mandated congregation.

As she wove through the crowd the boss took to the podium at the far end of the square. "I'm not going to count," he began, bestowing a smile upon his minions as Ted adjusted the microphone to his brother's height, "I'll *assume* all four hundred of you are here." He turned to his brother, "that right Ed? four hundred?"

"Minus the two guys from last week," Art hissed in Maggie's ear.

"What guys?"

"Bob Gianni and Alvaro Gutierrez. Curtains." Art propped his foot on the statue of Marley Moose and Maggie shook her head, neither names rang a bell, "Ted saw to it *personally*," he said, elbowing Maggie as the younger Harley brother stepped off the podium and stood to the side.

"And *I* say—" Milton expanded his chest and jabbed his cigarette at his troops, "if you lot don't like it then *ship the hell out.*"

"Guess it's too late for Bob and Alvaro," Art muttered. The men, Maggie was duly informed, had been dismissed at the end of last week, a sudden decision based on work quality—or so the official line went.

"Hush!" Maggie suppressed a grin, all the while maintaining her disapproval for Bob and Alvaro's misfortune and Art's disrespectful grumbling.

"It's come to my attention that you lot aren't happy campers," Milton gazed at his employees with an expression holding all the meaning in the world, "*some* of you aren't happy campers I oughta say…and evidently…"

"Spit it out," Art muttered.

"…evidently some of you are all uppity about *conditions*," Milton gestured to the extravagant Harley surrounds, the micro-metropolis built to further the studio's lofty aims, "this state-of-the-art complex I built for you all, the greatest technology money can buy—"

"Yeah yeah yeah we heard it all before—"

"Technology making for the greatest animation in the world, we're not just *any* studio, oh no…not just *a* studio. We're a *family*…"

"Well how do you like that? A *family*," Art laughed bitterly.

"We are." Maggie, suddenly aware their chatter was attracting attention, gazed at her shoes, shifting her toes inwards then splaying them out like a certain furry squirrel.

"You think success comes from nothing? From complaining about petty details? Well listen up and listen up good cause I'll tell you where success comes from…from hard work," Milton assumed a fierce expression and his body tightened like wire, "hard work and sacrifice—"

"I'd like to sacrifice you," Art said, scraping his shoe on the statue's base.

"Hey watch it," Maggie chided, all the while suppressing another grin. If the boss had something to say then they ought to be polite enough to listen.

"And seems it's not just the men who ain't happy…nope—some of my girls as well…or so I'm told." As Milton flicked his spent cigarette to the ground Maggie blanched.

"Communists," Art whispered, bending close to Maggie's ear. She stepped away from the heckler, tugging her ear to be rid of the tickle.

"Don't be fooled by that man in the White House!" Milton thundered as he pounded the podium with his fist, "that New Deal of his ain't a deal at all—I tell you what it is—it's a *raw* deal! A goddamned disgrace!"

"What bunk," Maggie said, her brow creased in anger.

"Mr *Roosevelt's* hell-bent on destroying men like me, men putting bread and butter on *your* table, men working for the good of our great country, men standing for dignity and livelihood—"

"Hey—" Maggie scowled, "that's not fair…"

"Troublemaker," Art said, leaning in even closer to deliver the accusation, "no point playing nice on account of your squirrel. Forget it—the guy can't stand competition see?"

After half-an-hour more of impassioned lecturing the crowd was finally free to leave, the boss apparently satisfied his talk had gone some way towards restoring faith. "Boy, that *really* burns me up," Harriet said, hurrying towards her friends with her mouth set in a line, "and if he thinks we'll fall for his snake-oil talks he got another thing coming."

"He said *awful* things," Maggie said, greatly angered by Milton's attack on their president.

"We got a new recruit?" Harriet asked Art.

"I got it on good account, she's a Communist."

"That'll do," Harriet laughed.

"I'm not a Communist."

"You know what one is?" Harriet asked, skeptical as always.

"Enough to know I'm not one of them."

"They eat babies and burn houses," Art made a face and licked his lips.

"And that's not the half of it," Harriet chimed in, enjoying herself for once, "they join unions and go out on strike."

"But you don't have enough support...do you?" Maggie looked at the ground and felt an anxious lurch. Milton was mad enough as it was, she hated to think what a strike might do to him, each day seemed to reveal more of his dark underbelly.

"Not yet," Harriet said, her eyes glinting, "but we will, I promise you that."

"Hey," Art turned to Harriet as the three of them left the courtyard, "tell Walt we oughta hit The Blue Note sometime."

"Sure. So long as you don't hit it too hard."

"Okay boss."

"Say, how bout a double-date?" Harriet danced her brows, an unusual spring in her step, "bring along your Communist."

"You like jazz?" Art said when Harriet had gone.

"Do I ever," Maggie lied. She frowned, wondering at her sudden compulsion to be agreeable for the sake of it.

"There's a band I'd like to take a look at—hear the singer's real keen."

"Wacky—" Maggie blurted out, immediately feeling rather silly to have done so.

"Wacky huh?" Art looked at her sideways, "you're really something else, you know that?"

"Oh I am, am I?"

She revved the Pussycat and frowned, not entirely sure about the spell she'd fallen under, the strange feeling she got whenever Art was around, the way she slumped a little to make herself less tall, told little white-lies about music she didn't much like.

Chapter Twelve

"Won't you join me?" Maggie instantly regretted her words. She hadn't seen much of Clara in the past few weeks, save for exchanging a few pleasantries in the censorious environment of Room 27C. Even Clara with her connections was expected to tow the line like the rest of them, or in Clara's own words, get that *goddamned orphan in that goddamned can.*

"Thing is the guy's crazy about me," Clara said, returning to her favorite topic of conversation. The last half-an-hour of their telephone call had been taken up with similar assertions regarding Milton's deeply held but rarely expressed feelings, "just don't show it easy you know?"

"Yes I'm sure that's what it is," Maggie said, consulting the paper and finding the antidote for her bad mood, "how about *The Roaring Twenties* with James Cagney?"

"The funny-looking fella?"

"Funny?" Maggie said, indignant on his behalf, "listen if we hurry along we'll make the seven o'clock session."

Two hours later Maggie and Clara left the half-empty theatre after an exciting foray into the world of bootlegging. "Humphrey Bogart ain't much neither," Clara said, issuing another of her blunt appraisals. She munched the last of her popcorn and

Maggie smirked, unable to deny her appreciation for the lady who never shied away from speaking her mind. "Old and ugly to boot."

"Aw, come on now—he's cute as a bug's ear," Maggie jibed, "and plenty rugged."

"You gotta be kidding," Clara guffawed, her eyes bugging out, "say, wanna come over?"

"Well…perhaps another time."

Maggie promised herself she'd follow through. After all Clara wasn't so bad, in fact the night had been rather fun—light-hearted—not peppered with pregnant pauses and talk of strikes and wars. "I got a whole house to myself," Clara boasted, "come on, live a little…pretty please…?"

Just last week Clara had left the women's hostel for good, a place positively teeming with women desperate to break into the movie business. Actresses, dancers or models—or all of the above as was generally the fate of long-legged women with big dreams. "What a dump," Clara rolled her eyes. She didn't miss it one bit. Especially the filthy drapes.

As if by magic a car pulled up at the curb and Clara skipped towards it. "Here he is, right on the knocker. Milton don't like me taking cabs," she explained proudly, "so George takes me wherever I want—dontcha George?" She rapped on the window and it wound down. "George, say hallo to Maggie—Maggie meet George." The driver nodded, stepped out of the car and squired Clara into it. She turned to Maggie with a wavering smile from the confines of the plush interior, "guess I won't be seeing you tomorrow."

"You're leaving Paint and Ink?"

"You bet I am. Course Milt wants me staying but I said to hell with that." She crossed her legs and draped her shapely self in a manner befitting the opulence of her carriage.

"But you'll miss having something to do, won't you?"

"Oh I got plenty to do. Spend the whole day in bed if I feel like it. Do what I damn-well please."

"The whole day," Maggie muttered as Clara departed in style, watched on by a group of movie patrons curious about the pedigree of the gorgeous fur-draped blonde.

Thrilled by the thought of the adventure ahead, Maggie turned the wheel and headed in the direction of her rendezvous with Ted. She'd dressed accordingly for the furtive excursion, dark pants and a rather drab blouse, a detail Clara had been quick to point out as they'd waited in line at the box-office. She'd considered donning a balaclava or kerchief to complete the outfit, but having nothing suitable to do the job, had decided against it in the end.

The Pussycat's door closed with a soft click and she sneaked through the lot, avoiding the danger of light-bathed paths. She'd been warned. There were guards patrolling the grounds and she would have to look smart. She gazed at the blocky buildings lit from below, the surreal statues of Harley heroes and row of palm trees no doubt shipped in at great expense. The effect was unreal, magical, as though the scene had been plucked from a Harley fantasy itself.

The grass squished underfoot as she crossed the lawn diagonally to Building A. She heard the sound of footsteps, a regular clacking coming closer and closer. Panicked, she dove behind a tree, crouching as the guard passed, his torch casting a frantic oval light in the black. Her heart thumped, her stomach in a tumble, and as he disappeared around a bend she leapt out and made a final dash to the steps.

Her back pressed against cool bricks as she sheltered in the shadow of the awning. A bat called out, swooping overhead, a screeching call followed by the flapping of wings. Then, more footsteps—not one set, but two. Flustered, she ducked under the railing and jumped, landing among the shrubs with a soft thud.

"You hear that?" said the man accompanying Ted. Maggie peered out, her senses alert, squatting on her haunches and holding her breath, frozen like a deer in the headlights but without the threat of an oncoming car. "We got a few rats maybe." The man stuck his foot in the bushes and gave it a half-hearted kick.

"Uh-huh, could be," Ted said loudly, aware his accomplice might come upon them at any moment. "Be sure and let me know if it leaks again okay? And any more mold, you know what to do."

"Yes sir, Mr Harley—best take a look before the rot sets in, least what I says anyways," the man said, pleased to impart his knowledge on such things.

"That's fine advice," Ted agreed.

"Matter of fact we get a lot of mold back home in Washington State."

"Uh-huh."

"Only thing does the trick is vinegar—that's right, vinegar."

"I'll take your word for it." Ted nodded and the man set off, tipping his cap.

"Good night Mr Harley."

"Night Leroy."

As Leroy's footsteps faded Maggie observed Ted from the safety of her shrubby hole. His hands burrowed in this pockets, the jiggling of coins distinct in the night air, his torso bent in a slight crescent. The light fell on his face, a stark geometry of light and dark from temple to collarbone.

"Ted," she called out softly. He turned as her head emerged from the shrubbery.

"Maggie?"

"You tell Leroy not to pick on small animals," she said in a loud whisper. He held out his hand and extricated the rather large rat, "why this *is* fun," she enthused, brushing her clothes before noting the tight expression at odds with her own.

"Shh." He put his finger to his lips, readying his keys for a speedy entrance.

The lights buzzed to life, a low hum flashing into a harsh, white glare. He removed the camera's dust cover and put it aside. "Where's it it go? Here?" Maggie asked as she extracted the canister from her bag.

The storekeeper had assured her of the film's quality. He'd been dubious at first, a woman buying film without the aid of a male chaperone, but she'd drawn him out on the subject and he'd finally come round—at last satisfied with her ability to make a tolerable decision.

"Good choice," Ted said, loading the film in the camera.

"Hold up—" Maggie rounded his shoulder to get a better view, "I missed that bit."

"Too late," he snapped the casing shut. "Next time."

There would have to be a next time. By Maggie's reckoning it would take no less than nine hours to complete the two-minute cartoon, a figure so shocking she'd been compelled to repeat her calculations twice more before really believing it. She lay the pile of sketches to her right and sat at the helm as Bill had.

"Fire away," Ted said, his initial anxiety gone. He pressed the green button and the machine jolted to life. She positioned the first sketch on the pegs and closed the glass plate on top, turning to Ted with a smile.

"Well here goes nothing." There was a click, then the sweet sound of film winding one frame closer to Lilly's grand debut. "One down, a couple thousand more to go."

It wasn't long before she got in the swing of it, her speed increasing by the minute as Ted stood by quietly. "Oh dammit!" She glared at the sketch with annoyance. A slight tear at the peg-hole was doing a capital job of throwing the whole thing out of whack.

"So that's her?" Ted said. She turned, a little startled, having almost forgotten her quiet accomplice.

"Uh-huh. Meet Squirrel Lilly, an adventurer and heroine of the highest order."

"That a leaf?"

"Leaf-boat."

"Beats me how you come up with these things—"

"Damnit!" she cussed again. Aligning the sketch with its damaged hole was proving almost impossible, "darn thing keeps slipping."

"Easy fixed," Ted said, opening a drawer and taking out a roll of narrow tape and pair of scissors.

"Why thank you Mr fix-it." She snipped off a length, swiftly repaired the damage and got back to work.

"She looks a little like you."

"Huh?"

"She—Lilly, she's a little like you..." He paused, perhaps worried he'd put his foot in it.

"Is she?" Maggie said, not at all offended by the comparison, "how do you figure that?"

"Let's see," he narrowed his eyes and considered the matter, "can't say for sure."

"Or perhaps it's safer you don't say," she laughed, "let me guess—is it the hairy feet or the buck teeth? Or perhaps her magnificent tail—" she broke off, suddenly aware of Ted's barometer-like cheeks, the red spreading upwards in a great, flooding rush. "I suppose there's no sense in you hanging about, I'll be quite all right here by myself...can't expect you to lose sleep on my account."

"Sure, all right." Ted frowned, unsure, then lay the key beside her and began writing instructions, how to remove the film without exposing it to light, how to switch off the power and turn the latch on the door.

"And I'll be sure and watch out for Leroy and his vinegar."

"Avoid the bushes," Ted agreed, a smile curving his lips as he jiggled his pockets, seemingly reluctant to leave. "I see what it is now," he gestured to Lilly, her squirrel features exploding with curiosity.

"It's in the eyes."

"Oh?" Maggie said, amused, "am I quite that manic?"

"Full of life."

"Wonderful, full of life," Maggie beamed, pleased with the compliment. "And *you* will be soon with any luck won't you Lilly? *We're* not afraid of Uncle Milt are we?" She rubbed her calf, slipped the next sketch from the diminishing pile and pressed the lever again. "I'll say one thing, that Bill must have one mighty strong leg—"

"You like music?" Ted said, abruptly changing tack, "jazz?"

Maggie froze, her foot hovering in mid-air. "Uh—" She pressed the lever with too much force and her foot slid from the metal and slapped to the floor, "well, no, not so very much." She frowned, confused as to whether she'd replaced the last sketch.

"How about the movies then?"

"Why yes...if you like." She looked over her shoulder as he bent to retrieve a slip of paper poking out from under a desk. He scowled, screwing it up and tossing it in the trash.

"What's that?"

"Propaganda...some fool stirring up trouble."

"Propaganda?"

She retrieved the crumpled ball and flattened it out. FIGHT FOR YOUR RIGHTS! it proclaimed in a bold, aggressive font. Her heart skipped a beat as she clocked the picture underneath, the photo of Milton from the *Los Angeles Times*—the horned, dragon-tailed monster she'd helped create. "Oh..." She scrunched the pamphlet up and returned to the machine with burning cheeks.

"How about Saturday…the movies?" The coins jiggled frantically as she composed her answer.

"So long as it's not a sappy romance—I do hate that kind of thing don't you?"

As Ted left Maggie to it she let out a noisy sigh, annoyed to have agreed to the date, especially to the movies. The last thing she wanted was him getting the wrong idea when there was no idea whatever to get. And the fact that Ted had invited her to sit next to him in a dark room, a place where feelings were better able to express themselves, only served to remind her that someone else had not.

Chapter Thirteen

"**N**ow let's see this place of yours," Maggie said as she, Harriet and Art pulled up outside the Bunker Hill mansion.

"*My* place…? You gotta be kidding." Harriet and Art exchanged amused looks.

"You never heard of a rooming-house?"

"Oh…I see," Maggie said, suddenly aware of the peeling paint, the rotting porch slats—not to mention her gaping naivety.

"Welcome to my mansion."

Harriet led the way in and the smell hit Maggie in a heady rush. Food, dust, and she guessed, the earthy smell of animal. Pets hadn't been allowed in the Goodwin household, her father thought it unhygienic, health being 'paramount to success and happiness', an expression that had soon lost popularity after Ellen Goodwin had taken ill.

"Owned by a Mr Goldstone," Harriet said, affecting a pompous voice, "lives in the Hollywood Hills and collects the rent while it rots to the ground."

"That's the plan," Art said, heading up the creaky staircase. Maggie grimaced as she followed, noting the peeling, yellowing wallpaper gaping at the joins.

"Someone ought to do something," she said, though what that thing might be she wasn't at all sure.

"Come and take in the view, madame," Harriet swirled her arm as they reached the second-floor and creaked down the dingy hallway. "Hallo Kitty," she bent to pet a starved, tortoiseshell cat. It arched his back and meowed loudly, its round eyes staring.

Inside Harriet and Walter's lodgings the smell changed subtly, from dusty and musty to dusty and yeasty. Conscious of the fug, Harriet flung the window open and turned with an anxious smile. "This is Walter," she nodded to the man in the ratty sofa-chair. "Walter?" Harriet said more loudly, "this is Maggie." His eyes flung open and he launched himself to his feet, extending his hand in greeting.

"How do you do," he croaked, clearing his throat before making his way across the room.

"How do you do. Goodness—what cold hands," Maggie said.

"What the hell time is it? You're late." Walter slapped Art's shoulder as he passed, yanked his coat from a hook and opened the door.

"We oughta fill our stomachs first," Harriet said, scooping the Lucky Strikes from the table and shoving them in her bag.

"Good idea—let's eat," Maggie agreed.

She'd been forewarned, The Blue Note was notorious for getting a little crazy. Especially if Art got loose with the dough. And that happened more often than not, Harriet explained with weary resignation. After one too many liquors the men would urge each other on, assuring each other of the harmlessness of just one more drink.

Art finished up his burger and smacked his lips. "Not your run-of-the-mill swing trash, nuh-uh," he thumbed at Maggie, grinning as he lit Walter's cigarette, "this one's nuts for swing."

"Yes I'm afraid I'm as dull as dishwater as far as music goes," Maggie said, feeling a little out. She dusted crumbs into a neat pile with her serviette, annoyed at Art's habit of poking fun at her preference for big-band mediocrity, the popular hits she couldn't even name when quizzed.

"Okay okay," Harriet said, coming to Maggie's defense, "so we know doodly-squat about this songbird of yours, big deal." She crossed her arms and suppressed a burp.

"Don't know Ella Marland?" Walter said as though they'd committed a capital offense, "where you girls been?"

"Busting our guts down at Paint and Ink is where," Harriet growled.

"And *how*." Maggie sighed, wiping mustard from her finger.

"First tour out West," Art went on, intent on sharing his dossier on the famous songbird. Maggie rested her chin in her hand, half-listening as Walter and Art waxed lyrical about something called syncopation.

"Okay folks," Harriet heaved herself out of the booth, "let's have at her."

The Blue Note wasn't much like The Palomar at all. Firstly it was much smaller, secondly it was much darker, and thirdly it was much smokier. But despite the lack of chandelier and grandeur and one-breasted ashtrays, the place felt cosy and intimate, and not the least bit cavernous or bland.

As the foursome fought their way to the bar Maggie held tight to Harriet's hand, "I can barely move," she shouted at the back of her friend's head. Art leaned into the bar and caught the bartender's attention and soon Maggie was furnished with a glass of sharp but sweet liquid. She gave Art the once-over as he directed Walter's attention to the stage....he did look like James Cagney—and wasn't funny-looking at all...

"Gin sling," Art shot her a wicked grin, a cigarette dangling from the corner of his mouth, "that'll fix you."

"Fix me will it?" She raised her eyebrows, "didn't figure I was broken."

"You get that pamphlet round the traps?" Walter said, eyeing Art as he downed a shot of whiskey. He wiped his mouth and rattled ice in the empty glass.

"Easy fella," Harriet muttered.

"Yep. Sure did," Art affirmed.

"Need any more?"

"One more run should do it."

"Two hundred do the trick?"

"That'll do." Art turned to Maggie and pointed at the stage, "that fella there's Arden Johnson."

"I see."

"Best drummer this side of Texas."

"Oh yeah?" Walter challenged, "you forget Joel Hargrove or something?"

"Fair point."

Soon the gin sling started in on its fixing and Maggie felt threads loosen, all at once at ease in the enforced intimacy of the tiny club. "You get one?" Art said, passing over the familiar slip of paper, "our little masterpiece?" Maggie froze.

"Uh-huh. I saw it," she sniffed, holding the pamphlet loosely.

"Walt's been real busy with the ditto machine," he prodded Maggie's ribs, "what gives? You don't like it?"

"You might have said that's all," she folded the pamphlet briskly and returned it.

"Okay I get it," Art turned to Walter, "this one wants to play in the mud *and* keep her hands clean…found a real nice spot on the fence." He shook his head sadly then waved the pamphlet at her, "thought you'd be okay with it, your squirrel and my raccoon being so close and all."

"That's not fair—"

"I'll tell you what's not fair, getting fired for no good reason is what." Walter slung his arm round Harriet's shoulder and kissed the top of her head, "works like a dog this one—it's criminal."

"Yeah but joining a union ain't," Harriet said, her eyes narrowing, "not any more."

"Step out of line and you'll know about it." Walter's jaw ground like a millstone and he drew a finger across his throat.

"Now hold up just a minute, this isn't some gangster movie," Maggie protested.

"One thing's for sure, we got 'em spooked." Harriet glanced at Maggie, who, disappointed they'd returned to the subject of striking once again, examined her gin sling with exaggerated interest.

"That fancy camera still bust?" Walter asked as Art ordered more drinks, "or they too dumb to figure the thing out."

"Too dumb," Harriet smirked.

"Another forty grand down the plug-hole."

"The bastard's as stubborn as it comes…used to be you could talk to the guy," Art scowled as Walter pointed to the stage.

"Here comes trouble—"

They turned to the bright lights. To Ella Marland, magnificent in shimmering silver gown, her hand at the microphone as she spoke in husky tones, "good evening ladies and gentlemen— you all enjoying yourselves out there?"

"You bet!" Walter called out. He put his fingers to his lips and let out a piercing whistle.

"Shush!" Harriet bounced her hip against his, smiling despite herself. She clapped her hands and blew a whistle of her own.

"Thank you, thank you everyone—"

As the drums set to a steady-handed trill the songbird closed her eyes and began to sing. Art, close by Maggie's side, tapped his feet as the double bass joined in. "*Do da de da da da de…*" Fearing there was no hope of understanding the alien rhythm, Maggie gripped her glass as Art leaned in. She felt his breath on her cheek and caught the scent of hair-lotion, cigarettes and liquor.

"You look as if you're doing math," he teased, moving her shoulders to and fro as the songbird warbled on, "relax, just go with the flow." His arm encircled her waist as the melody bounded erratically from note to note, but a moment later he let it drop, his attention returning to the stage.

By the night's end Maggie had at least begun to understand one thing. When it came to jazz you had to forget about making sense of anything. Jazz, according to Art, was the antithesis of predictability. Jazz was music for the fearless, for the brave, "for people who believe in freedom and art," he shouted above the ruckus as they sat at a dark table. He threw back his head and emptied the last of his whiskey, seemingly at the end of the heart-felt soliloquy.

"You sound just like Uncle Milt," Maggie said, "preaching from your pulpit." Art mopped his forehead with a serviette and leveled her a cool look.

"That bastard can go to hell," he hissed, banging his glass on the table. Maggie, caught off-guard and somewhat shocked, recoiled as he pushed back his chair and made his way to the bar.

"Oh my…" Maggie said, turning to Harriet for answers.

"He's full of booze," she said, waving her hand dismissively, "don't take it serious."

"Oh yeah, sure, that's right," Walter snorted, suddenly turning on his wife, "just full of booze, just a *useless* drunk. I'll have you know Art's got damned-good reason to be mad as hell."

"Walter spill the beans yet?" Art said a few minutes later when he'd returned with more whiskey.

"No. What beans?" Maggie said, shaking her head as though to clear it.

"Beans, peanuts, all good for counting," Walter said bitterly. He lit another cigarette, the flame dangerously close to his nose.

"Got myself demoted," Art leaned in to catch the flame then slapped out a beat on the barrel of his chest.

"What?" Maggie exclaimed.

"Bastard's put me on as an in-betweener."

"What the hell is that anyways?" Walter took a drag on his cigarette then passed it to Harriet.

"That's easy," Maggie began, rising to the occasion, "you see you got the keyframes, the main sketches—"

"The big boys job—" Art interjected.

"Then between them you got all these other ones, see —*between* them."

"Swell," Walter drawled, unimpressed.

"Well I think it is," Maggie said, turning to Art with sympathy, "I'm awful sorry—"

"Won't be long before he shows you the door," Walter predicted.

"So what," Art shrugged, "I got options."

"But you used to be friends," Maggie insisted, recalling an article filed away in her scrap-book. After finding success with his early cartoons, Milton Harley had taken on the bright-eyed bushy-tailed Art, fresh out of art school and eager to fill the role of underling. Not long after that the great Wild Willie had been conceived.

"Friends? Oh yeah sure, we go way back."

"So much for loyalty," Maggie folded her arms and shook her head slowly.

"Next thing he'll have me coloring in with you gals."

"Now hold on, I won't have you making fun of our work," Maggie warned.

"Why not? You sure as hell do," Art said with a sly smile.

It was true and Maggie shrank from the memory of her words —the work was deadly-dull and required little more than a steady hand and the ability to tell red from green.

"What'd you call it? Now that's right—A hellhole, wasn't it?" Art's eyes narrowed and he threw back his head to retrieve the last drops of amber liquid, "thought you were desperate to do something more *intelligent?*"

"All the same," Maggie glanced at Harriet anxiously, "I'm terribly fond of everyone—"

"It's our very own little hellhole," Harriet said, emitting a gigantic yawn, "last one," she called out as Walter left for one more battle-weary trek to the bar.

"I'm not about to up and leave," Maggie said, "leave the Orphan in the lurch."

"She's loyal." Art scooted his chair close, draped an arm about her shoulders and addressed Harriet, "better keep an eye on that husband of yours." Harriet rolled her eyes, and eager to put an end to the evening, went off to hurry him along.

Maggie stiffened as Art's face came towards hers. She felt the tip of his nose brush her jaw, and, experiencing a torrent of mixed emotions, averted her face at the last instant. "Maybe not," he said, relaxing his hold and shifting his attention to Harriet and Walter, returning from the bar with one for the road and one for *another* road.

"It was him I swear—" Walter yelled above the drunken chatter of stragglers unwilling to put an end to their evening. Maggie rubbed her ears, still suffering the effects of the confounding jazz. "I swear," Walter repeated as he plonked himself down unsteadily.

"Uh-oh," Harriet balked at the sight of the cosy couple, "not interrupting anything are we…?"

"Nope," Art removed his arm completely and shook the last cigarette from his pack, "not a thing…all completely innocent."

"It *was* him," Walter insisted, continuing to argue the point with his wife, whatever that point was.

"Yeah, yeah, keep your hat on," Harriet snapped.

"What you lovebirds fighting about?" Art regarded the couple in his usual sardonic way and Maggie, smiling to hide her mounting confusion, wondered if he'd bother to make another advance before the night was done. In the face of her own rather conflicted feelings he seemed rather too calm about the matter. She suddenly wished she *had* kissed him.

Walter, unable to convince his wife of whatever it was she refused to believe, turned to Art for support. "Of all the low blows," he said, shaking his head and thumbing at the back of the club, "of all the low blows…"

"What? They run out of hooch?" Art smirked.

"We got a spy in the joint," Walter revealed, leaning in to convene with Art, "a dirty stinking spy."

"Don't listen to him, he's paranoid," Harriet said with an impatient sigh.

"Wouldn't put it past him," Art said, siding with his friend.

"Put *what* past *who*?" Maggie demanded.

"The spy," Harriet scoffed.

"What spy?"

"Your Ted that's who." Walter stared at Maggie coldly.

"He's not *my* Ted at all," she said, turning to search the crowd, "and I very much doubt Ted would *spy*."

"Heard you two been getting a little familiar?" Walter sneered.

"That's right," Art confirmed, "*real* cosy."

"Hey—" Harriet shot Art a warning look, "mind your manners wiseguy."

"I'm not getting cosy *or* familiar," Maggie said, suddenly wishing she'd accepted Ted's offer to sneak into the camera-room that very evening. Instead she'd concocted a flimsy excuse, an imaginary headache and upset stomach—and a desire to stay very much in bed. "Ted wouldn't spy on us, that's ridiculous."

"He'll do whatever big brother says—yes sir, no sir," Walter grumbled.

"But…?" she looked to Harriet for support, "would he?"

"Who knows what dirty tricks they'll pull, all's fair in love and war…wasn't him anyways—"

"Was," Walter insisted.

"Nu-uh."

"You didn't see him—*I* did," Walter nursed his drink, sulking as Harriet massaged his neck.

"Come on pal, lets wrap it up."

Maggie kept a sober eye on the road as they drove to Bunker Hill. Art had turned down her offer to get behind the wheel, but it wasn't the first time she'd been escorted home by a boozy date. If worse came to worst, Maggie figured, she could always take hold of the wheel and reach over with her long leg to step on the brake.

"Tally-ho," Harriet called out, waving royally as she and Walter said their goodbyes. Since uncovering Maggie's assumptions about their living conditions the kidding had been relentless.

"Tally-ho," Maggie called back in good humor.

"Better take her home to bed," Harriet advised Art with a wink, "a girl needs her beauty sleep you know—hey! Whoa there fella—" she caught Walter as he stumbled at the door, "keep it down will ya? We're in enough strife as it is."

Maggie and her ossified companion remained silent on the drive to Huntington Park. She'd decided he *would* try to kiss her again. Now they had more privacy. He'd escort her to the gate, remove his hat and repeat the performance with better results.

"Not quite a mansion…but not bad for starters," Art said, appraising her apartment as they pulled up at the curb.

"I don't require a mansion."

"No?"

"No."

"But you're working on it right? Good for you I say, go get him—go get your Harley." Art shot her a crooked smile as the car idled in the quiet. Fire rose in her throat and she waited for an apology, but none came, instead he tapped on the dash-board and whistled a tune. "That Ella sure was something huh?" he said, finally meeting her gaze.

"I suppose so, if you like," she flung the door open and stepped out onto the sidewalk, "good night."

"Tally-ho."

He waved, taking off into the night, a single definitive slice through the still, desert air.

Chapter Fourteen

There was no escape. She was trapped, dressed from head to toe in black and teetering at the edge of a three-story drop. The cartoon scattered behind her, pages spiraling in a whirlwind. Lilly, fighting to captain the flimsy vessel, screamed from the bow, "tally-ho, tally-ho!" There was nothing else for it. Maggie jumped, and for a moment she floated, suspended in the air before plummeting in a stomach-churning rush—

She gasped, waking with a jolt and lying still as reality returned…the emerald-green patchwork bedspread, the pretty three-legged walnut nightstand, the square of sunlight folding like origami from ceiling to wall to floor…and out the window, the familiar backdrop of cloudless blue sky.

She dressed briskly, keen to sweep away the memory of Art's accusations…he thought her a gold-digger but she was nothing of the sort. Grand houses and chauffeurs meant nothing to her. And as for the other bone of contention between them, she had no beef whatever with unions or striking or standing up for one's rights, in fact her father had been instrumental in passing the Wagner Act through Congress. Just as Art was free to exercise his right to strike she too was free to follow her own path, and if that meant remaining neutral on the matter then so be it. "So be it," she declared as a car-horn sounded from the street.

She straightened her hat and bounded downstairs. "Get in," Clara's perfect face poked from the window and Maggie addressed the driver.

"No need for assistance George," she said, opening the door as Clara scooted over.

"Aw let the guy do his job will ya?"

"Yeah I might get bored," George said as they took off at a leisurely pace. Clara frowned at Maggie's hat.

"What you wearing *that* for?"

"Well I don't know," Maggie said curtly, not in the mood for teasing—having already suffered a gut-full from her friends the night before, "why does anyone wear a hat?" she added as she settled into the luxury of leather and lacquered wood.

"Oh I dunno—maybe you got no hair or something?" Clara jiggled her pin-thin brows. "So? We gonna be sisters or what?" She jabbed George's shoulder as they turned into Soto Street, "I said the *long* way, dummy." She shook her head and rolled her eyes at his mistake, "he'll grow on you—if ya let him."

"That's what they all say," their chauffeur said with a smile.

"Oh yeah?" Clara slapped his shoulder and turned to Maggie, "you coming to the shindig? Now she's in the can you can take a breather."

"In the can? What, the Orphan?"

"Shh—" Clara bit her lip guiltily, "keep it on the lowdown will ya?"

"But why are we still busting our guts if—"

"*I* dunno—cause Milt says so okay?" She lit a cigarette, "why you have to ask so many questions—you don't want me getting in trouble do ya?"

"Of course not, but if she's done then why don't we know about it?"

"Aw forget it will ya? Thought you said you wanna have fun?"

"I do."

"Good. Atta girl. Here—cigarette?"

To Maggie's surprise, smoking wasn't anywhere near as diffi-cult as she'd imagined, and the smell not nearly so bad. She watched the tip glow a fierce orange-red, coughed, then passed it back to the expert.

"Look," Clara said. She blew a series of perfect smoke-rings then broke them with a poke of her nose.

"Bravo!" Maggie applauded, genuinely delighted at Clara's trick.

"Milt don't like it, thinks it's cheap."

"But it takes skill."

"Yeah, sure it does," Clara said, suddenly downcast as Maggie wound down the window and let the air in.

They left the winding road, turning into a steep driveway cut through pockets of greenery. Here and there palm trees swayed among stouter trees. "It's the cat's meow," Clara observed in a fashionable monotone as they approached Milton Harley's most generous gift to date, the rent-free house in the Hollywood hills. "Used to be Lulu Daly's," she explained, tossing her keys in a glass bowl as they entered, "whoever the hell that is." She went to the kitchen in search of supplies for their morning soirée then led her guest to the patio, glasses and champagne in hand.

"Will you get a load of that..." Maggie gawped at the spec-tacular view—not to mention the adorable peanut-shaped pool winking in the morning sun. "But it's only eleven o'clock, don't you have any...tea?" she asked, secretly hoping Clara wouldn't, and wondering at her odd request—she hadn't touched the nasty stuff since the Goodwins had packed their trunks and left London for good.

"Tea, shmee," Clara popped the champagne without losing a drop.

"Bravo," Maggie said, once again impressed with her host's prowess.

"Beats me why some folks slop it about." She put Maggie's glass on the balustrade and filled it to the brim, "up to you, take it or leave it."

"I'll take it." Maggie chimed her glass to Clara's and they drank champagne at eleven in the morning without a care in the world.

"I haven't a care in the world," Clara said, sipping and smoking as she paraded about her dominion. She pointed to a Spanish-style mansion nestled in an oasis on the adjacent canyon, "see?" Clara smiled mischievously, "play your cards right and that one's yours."

"Oh…Ted's house?"

"You betcha," she angled Maggie's body for a better view, "not that one, dummy—the other one, there, with the fountain and all."

"Ah—now I see it," Maggie said, clapping eyes on the white-washed colossus with arched balconies and endless rooms, the gigantic pool surrounded by candy-colored deck-chairs, the zigzag of terraced lawns leading down to a private nook. "Wonderful," Maggie sighed, closing her eyes and picturing herself lounging about in the pool and suspecting Ted might look rather nice in a bathing-suit—what with his broad shoulders and all…

The sound of the telephone rang out. "That'll be Milt," Clara exclaimed as she ran inside, clacking over marble tiles like a miniature donkey—Italian tiles, Maggie had been informed. "He always telephones at lunch," Clara called over her shoulder, as though the information were vital to them both.

Art on the other hand was acting like a heel, Maggie decided as Clara attended to her lover in the living room, her face soft and dreamy as she cradled the receiver to her creamy cheek. "He's in a good mood," Clara said a while later as she stretched out on a deck-chair and made her companion to do the same. Maggie, without the benefit of sunglasses, squinted at her glass, the bubbles rising to the surface, their paths fixed yet fluid like birds on the wing.

"You're happy," Maggie said, suddenly wondering if it would be so bad after all, living the high-life without a care in the world, clacking about in heels and popping champagne in the middle of the day.

"You bet I am." Clara snapped open a case and removed a pair of over-sized sunglasses, "who wouldn't be with a guy like Milt."

"Well, there's tomatoes and there's tomatoes—"

"—let's call the whole thing off! Hey, you hungry?"

"Starved."

"George! *George!*" Clara yelled, springing to her feet, "taking a nap I bet."

They ate heartily, an eclectic array. Having left George in peace to arrange the spread herself, Clara went on to declare each of the delicacies her most favorite food in the whole wide world.

"They can't all be your favorite," Maggie pointed out logically.

"Why the hell not?"

"Sure," Maggie chuckled, "why the hell not."

So, with Maggie's permission, peaches were superseded by ice-cream, ice-cream by peanut butter, peanut butter by roast-chicken, roast-chicken by oranges. "But no vegetables," Clara said in a tone reminiscent of Milton's. She caught Maggie's eye and grinned, "I *won't* abide by vegetables." She just wouldn't have it.

"Sure beats soda-biscuits and coffee," Maggie said, demolishing the last of her rosy-skinned peach. She licked her fingers clean and started in on the chicken.

"Thing is you gotta get smart."

"I guess you're right," Maggie said, suddenly exhausted as Clara topped up her glass. The food had made her sleepy, or more likely it was the drink, and staying in bed all day seemed like the best thing in the world just now. She eyed Clara enviously, the beautiful woman gnawing a chicken wing who'd broken free from underpaid, undervalued work, not to mention noisy hostels with filthy drapes. Perhaps it *would* be easier to take a turn at easystreet and forget about grand ambitions…besides, Maggie mused, fingering her glass uneasily, bubbles always burst when they reached the surface, disappeared as if they'd never even existed.

"Goddamned Orphan," Maggie muttered. Clara waved her finger, nodding smugly.

"Knew you'd see what's good for you, forget all that slaving. Take the easy road."

Maggie, suddenly snapping out of her inertia, sprang to her feet, ashamed at her shirking—even if it was in thought only. "Nope, what's good for me is getting on in the world, doing what I love—"

"Sure but you gotta play the game *some*. Shoot—it's Milt!" Clara sat bolt upright and stared in the direction of the Rolls-Royce, arriving, as promised, right after lunch.

Chapter Fifteen

*A*part from her aching calf, now settled into stiffness, Maggie felt surprisingly refreshed after only three hours sleep. But there'd been a disappointing surprise awaiting her in the dead of night in Harley's carpark. Instead of Ted she'd been met by Leroy, the groundsman with the fondness for vinegar. He'd escorted her to Building A, handed over the keys and delivered a message from her absent accomplice. Circumstances had dictated Ted's absence, and if Miss Goodwin so happened to find Mr Harley out of the office when returning the key at her earliest convenience, then she ought slip it under the door in an envelope, in the interests of safe-keeping.

The morning passed at snail's-pace down at Paint and Ink. More leaves and trees and confounding blades of grass. She glared at the goddamned Orphan and recalled Clara's slip of the tongue. Why the hell were they still laboring away when the golden-locked princess-to-be was supposedly in the can?

"Just say I sent you, okay?" Harriet whispered in Maggie's direction. Roy, a former friend of Walter would set Maggie's little film in the right direction down at processing, make sure it fell into the right hands.

"Thank you," Maggie said, glancing at the clock and feeling for the key in her pocket.

She rapped on the door, reading the brass plate as she entered. "So that's what you are, Chief Production Manager huh?" Maggie stood expectantly at Ted's desk, taking in the surrounds with bright interest. "Why," she laughed, noting the oversized desk and ostentatious chair, "it's exactly like Milton's. You're twins."

"Leroy found you all right then?" He looked up from his papers briefly.

"Uh-huh," she took the key from her pocket and placed it gently on the desk, "I didn't have an envelope so guess I'm lucky you're in."

"I guess," he knocked a pile of papers on end and placed the bundle to the side.

"Lilly's done—well so far so good—oh and I've a contact down at processing," she said with a wink.

"Swell," he muttered, eager to return to business.

"Swell, yes," Maggie said, rattled by his somber mood. He seemed rather aloof…irritated even, "you haven't been found out have you? I've kept my side of the bargain, not a word." She caught her cheek in her teeth at her white-lie, "say, you've a terrific pool up there in the hills, you see we had a little picnic and a swell time spying—Clara's a veritable expert on the Harley brothers, matter of fact I think she oughta run a tour bus. Oh and I smoked a cigarette—well only a puff or two…"

Ted's expression seemed set. Unamused, cold, and the mention of his glorious home had done nothing to lift his spirits like she thought it would. "Poor Clara. I feel a little sorry for her waiting around all day for the telephone to ring."

"Poor Clara?" Ted looked up, an angry frown marking his

brow, "poor Clara's hit the jackpot." Maggie, startled by his bitter tone, felt a lick of anger. She'd had quite enough of men telling women what they could or couldn't have and how they might go about getting it.

"Milton's got what he wants so why not Clara?" Her heart thudded as she stood awkwardly, her torso twisted as though meaning to leave but not quite following through, "anyways, we should all do as we please…and, as it happens, I'd very much like to go to the movies with you," she said, sure that would do the trick, snap Ted out of his mood. "Tonight? I'm free if you are," she trailed a finger along the surface of the twin desk, "are you a Bogart or Cagney man?"

"Neither," he said without hesitation.

"Neither?" she recoiled in mock horror, grabbed the newspaper on his desk and flicked through to the entertainment pages. "Let's see now, how about *Time to Die*? You won't find either of them in that…"

"I'll be out of town a while."

"Oh…I see. A raincheck then."

"Maybe a few weeks," he rubbed his nose and shifted a folder out the way to make way for another.

"Well when you're back…after all you've done for me and Lilly—"

"That how you feel is it?" Ted's brow drew tight and his eyes flashed. He cleared his throat and swiped the key from the desk.

"Why yes, I—"

"I got enough business to attend to as it is," he said, shuffling more papers, "besides I don't go much in for the movies."

"Oh…"

"Way I see it we're even."

Maggie left the office with a tight chest. As if she'd swallowed a golf ball and there was nowhere for it to go. What had happened to the sweet, kind, eager-to-please Ted who blushed at the slightest provocation? *Don't care for the movies?* Maggie fumed, reeling from the shock of his coldness as she rushed downstairs. *What bunk.* After all, she was only complying with what he'd wanted in the first place. His sudden change of heart just didn't feel right—and it sure as hell didn't feel familiar, getting the brushoff like that.

Chapter Sixteen

F ear gripped her heart. "What on earth do you mean *not* here?" Three days had passed since she'd sneaked her film to Roy at the little window down at processing, but now, it seemed, Roy had been replaced with someone else.

"I mean it ain't here," said the man who wasn't Roy, regarding Maggie with suspicion.

"Well check again would you?"

"Listen lady, if it ain't here, it ain't here."

"But Roy said…you *do* know Roy don't you?"

"Sure I know him."

"It's awful important."

"Well if it's so important then how come I ain't heard about it?" He turned, checking the reels in the shelf behind him, "nope. No cigar, nothing for a Maggie. What's the last name?"

"Oh, no no—forget it," Maggie said as he heaved a ledger onto the counter.

"What day you say? Three days ago was it?"

"No I'm afraid we—Roy didn't have time to write it down."

She left in a panic. What if the thing had been lost? Or worse still if Roy had been found out…? More likely it was just a case of the studio running behind schedule, Maggie told herself as she scowled at the dreaded clock. Only two minutes left to scurry back to jail.

She slowed, the urge to dawdle suddenly trumping her reflex to obey and submit to all things Harley. She would take her time, goddammit. To hell with Sergeant Mary and her tight-faced barking. In fact, Maggie mused with rising indignation, this little Miss goody-two-shoes didn't feel like obliging at all. On the contrary, she had a mind to skip the entire afternoon of drudgery and go straight on home to bed. Forget all about silly orphans and men who turned to ice for no good reason.

She marched into Paint and Ink, her defiance palpable. "Good afternoon everyone," she sang out, in no mood to be contrite.

"What's got into you?" Harriet hissed, clearly impressed by her friend's new attitude.

"Lilly's gone missing," Maggie shot back as the sergeant approached, evidently to to deliver a dose. Mary's hands clasped in a tense knot as she stared down her nose.

"Maggie—Mr Harley wants to see you in his office."

"No he doesn't," Maggie muttered, momentarily confused. She stabbed her paintbrush in the paint and baulked, "oh you mean Milton?"

"Of course I mean Milton," Mary said, thoroughly annoyed, "and now you've had the goodness to show up you'd better hop to it—come along now."

Maggie rose to her feet stiffly, her urge to rebel gone. A chill gripped her heart, her fears mounting rapidly at the thought she'd been found out.

Minutes later, light-headed and terrified, she stood at Milton's office, eyeing his brother's den over the way—the murky shape moving behind the pane of rippled glass. Ted, attending to *business* she supposed. As she sniffed away wounded pride she heard the sound of raised voices...

All of a sudden the door swung open and Art stormed out, his eyes unseeing and jaw set in a tight square. He turned to Maggie for an instant before marching away, his head shaking in dismay.

"Come in," Milton growled, motioning for Maggie to enter, "I said *come in*, Miss Goodwin." She gulped, preparing to face whatever punishment the great man had in mind—working twenty-four hours a day without pay for example. "Sit," he gestured to the seat she'd occupied four months ago, back when she'd believed in the wholesale goodness of the studio boss. He pushed his cigarettes away then changed his mind, hooking them back with his fingertips and shaking one free, "cigarette?"

"No…thank you," she gnawed her cheek as he inhaled a lungful of white wisps and waved his hand about.

"Helps me relax, gives me room to think."

"Yes. I see," Maggie squeaked.

"Schrieber didn't run you over?"

"No. I'm quite all right thank you."

"I believe he's a confidant of yours, am I right?" he raised his brow in a question.

"Confidant? I don't know about that…I'm not a Communist if that's what you're thinking."

"Not mixed up in this union business?"

"I won't strike."

"No?"

"No Mr Harley, I promised to work hard and that's what I'm doing, *will* do, and as far as Mr Schrieber is concerned—well there is no concern…we're friends, and that's the long and the short of it."

"So…no romantic involvement?"

"No," Maggie said stiffly, thinking it was none of his business and recalling a fellow Paint and Inker's recent dilemma, either accept a long-awaited marriage proposal or keep her job—she couldn't have both it seemed.

"What about this Harriet person, Harriet Mueller? She a friend of yours too?"

"Yes," Maggie said warily, "she is."

"And friends stick together wouldn't you say?" he ground his half-smoked cigarette into the ashtray.

"But you see Mr Harley," Maggie began carefully, "friends don't always swim in the same ocean. Or ride the same boat."

"Or eat the same plankton?"

"Exactly so," Maggie said, wondering if he was merely toying with her before delivering the final blow. She felt a hot rush of indignation, an urge to defend her fellow Paint and Inkers, besides, she figured, if she was about to feel the full force of Milt's boot she may as well go out swinging. "Mr Harley…do you know some of us Paint and Ink girls have never been to see the rushes? Not *ever*."

"That a fact?"

"Yes it is. And I think the system ought to be fairer. You ought to listen to our views, take them into consideration—even if we are the so-called weaker sex," her heart raced, adrenaline rushing from head to toe and back again.

"Equality for every man, eh?"

"That's right." She searched for signs Milton might explode in a rage, but there was no jaw-clenching, eye-twitching or tell-tale rattle-snake pose…

"No favors? Is that what you're proposing?"

"I'm only saying we live in a democracy, it's what this country stands for after all—"

"Never mind what the country stands for!" He slapped the desk and she shrank away, feeling sick at the thought that Ted might have betrayed her.

"What is it you wanted to see me about Mr Harley?" she murmured, preparing herself as best she could for the inevitable fall of the axe.

"I have a proposal."

"Proposal?" She looked up, blinking, her brow furrowed as his words sunk in.

"You need your ears cleaned out or something? That's what I said, a proposal."

Her heart stood still as her thoughts broke free and raced to rosier conclusions…*proposal?* Perhaps he wasn't about to seal her fate with a swift kick after all, "not romantic I hope," she blundered, her nerves getting the better of her. He frowned, clearly irritated and she clamped her mouth shut.

"You want to hear it or not?"

"Very much so—*yes.*"

"Post-production starts next week," he cleared phlegm from his throat and continued, "signed off last night as a matter of fact."

"So she *is* in the can," Maggie muttered. Milton squinted, cupping his ear.

"What? Speak up—"

"She's finished? Thank-goodness for that," Maggie said with a noisy sigh of relief.

Finally. There'd be no more finicky forest leaves, no more blonde curls—and no more pesky birds alighting on impossibly-fine twigs with their impossibly-fine legs. "You really oughtn't keep us in the dark like that—good gracious—we had no idea if the damned thing would *ever* end."

"Now that's a fine way to talk about our Orphan—"

"Oh no she's *lovely*—"

"Never mind that." He fiddled with his sleeve, shoved a familiar-looking package across the desk and leaned back to observe its effect.

Color drained from Maggie's face as the realization hit home. She licked her lips, her mouth dry as sand. Instinct told her swipe her squirrel and bolt from the room without looking back, but as she leaned forward to claim her he shifted the package out of reach.

"I…" Maggie began, utterly at a loss for words. He held up his hand.

"I don't want to know how you managed it."

"But…you saw her?" Maggie's eyes widened, "my squirrel?"

"That's right."

"You saw my Lilly?"

"Don't go getting ahead of yourself. She needs work and lots of it. We'll go over the details later, arrange a meeting or something." She folded her hands in her lap, stunned at the incredible turn of events as he drummed his fingers on the desk, "but in the meantime I'm looking for an extra pair of hands, an in-betweener who won't get distracted, think you're up to the task?"

"Oh Mr Harley!" Maggie gasped, her head in a wonderful spin, "I sure am!"

"Tally-ho!" Maggie hurried toward her friends, lined up in the cafeteria for lunch, "the Orphan's *over* folks—she's in the can!"

"Yeah we heard," Dora said, regarding her cooly.

"Let's just hope she don't escape," Harriet said as they reached the counter and saw the feast supplied to celebrate the milestone. Baked-bean sandwiches and fresh beef-tongue, shrimp aspic with Thousand Island dressing and just about as much damned spam as you could fit on your plate—and in Harriet's case, Maggie joked, that amounted to at least two tins.

"Now we can *all* start over, start something new," she enthused as they claimed their usual table in the shade.

"So what did he want?" Dora asked, "don't keep us in suspense."

"You in trouble?" Harriet looked up as she started in on her caramel tea-roll.

"Oh no…not at all," Maggie teased a shrimp from its jellied surrounds, waiting for the right time to reveal her astounding news.

"He say anything about us?"

"What do you mean?"

"He ask about any of us Communists?" Dora and Harriet shared a furtive glance.

"No..." Maggie trailed her fork through the aspic in search of more shrimp, "why?" she said, beginning to feel more than a little sheepish. Harriet snorted.

"To figure out when the enemy's gonna strike—literally."

"When?" Maggie looked up, alarmed.

"Better watch what we say," Dora warned, "she's hitched her horse to the golden pole."

"I've done nothing of the sort," Maggie hit back as they regarded her with amusement laced with contempt, "and if you mean Ted you couldn't be more wrong—"

"Come on Mags," Harriet grumbled, "give over—no-one gets a meeting with Milt for nothing."

"You won't believe it Hattie...I did it!" Maggie burst out, unable to contain herself any longer, "I did it..."

"Did what? Don't say you got us a pay rise?"

"Milton saw my squirrel and well...I guess I just got promoted!"

"Wha—" Dora's mouth hung open.

"That's right. The very first lady-animator at Harley Studios."

"Holy Moly..." Harriet joined Dora in open-mouthed astonishment.

"I can hardly believe it myself," Maggie admitted, her eyes shining with emotion.

"Guess you won't be joining us now," Dora said, her delivery flat. Maggie looked at her plate, her appetite waning.

"No but I'm blazing the way for the rest of you—"

"Yeah I bet, right to the top." Dora shook her head and they fell into an uncomfortable silence.

"Perhaps if you tried a little harder you might get somewhere too," Maggie said, immediately regretting her words, "—sorry, I didn't meant that—"

"So that's how you're gonna play it is it?" Dora said, standing abruptly and storming off, disgusted at Maggie's cheap shot.

She replaced the receiver and stared at her reflection, her wild excitement tempered by fatigue—and something else too. Melancholy. Since her run-in with Dora and Harriet earlier that day she'd been feeling more alone than she cared to admit. Her suggestion she and Harriet go bowling had been turned down flat. It seemed her closest friend within three-thousand miles was otherwise engaged.

She dialed the New York exchange and waited for the familiar click. "Hallo Paps," Maggie said in the loud voice she thought necessary for long-distance connections, "can't talk long but I've marvelous news—the most marvelous news in the world." She relayed the day's surprising events and her father, suitably delighted and not the least bit surprised, thought his daughter the most tenacious young lady he'd ever had the pleasure of knowing, if only she'd come home for a visit then life would be just about perfect. "I will Paps, at Christmas."

An hour later she changed position. From the corner of the sofa to the foot of her bed. From the foot of her bed to the hallway again. She stared at the telephone, her need for company outweighing pride.

She dialed the number and waited anxiously. "Maggie?" he said, "that you? I thought about calling."

"Did you?" Her spirits lifted, "I'm glad, you see after The Blue Note I—" she held off, there was no need to go over the particulars. "I've terrific news—but I suppose you know."

"Uh huh."

"But isn't it marvelous?"

"Congratulations."

"Oh it'll be swell, gabbing all day about pencils—and yammering too if you like."

"Nope."

"Oh come now," Maggie chided, "don't say you're snubbing me too, now I'm on the up and up?"

"Guess Milt needs loyal men—even if they are ladies," Art mumbled, as though distracted by something—or someone else.

"Pardon?"

"He's knocking us troublemakers off, one by one."

Maggie frowned at the receiver, kicking herself for not putting two and two together sooner. "Oh Art...he didn't fire you did he?" She stared at the doodle she'd scribbled on the back of an envelope, a Medusa-like creature with bloodied fangs. She scrawled over the top and tossed the pencil aside, "Milt's a a fool, a *complete* fool."

"I'll get over it."

"What's say we hit the town, have a drink or two?" Maggie, straining to hear more clearly, was sure she heard a woman's voice in the background, "or bowling, bout time I faced the music."

"I'm still recovering from last night. Anyways, there's a meeting I gotta be at."

"Oh. More organizing?"

"Uh-huh. You interested?"

She supposed she *could* go, if only for the sake of company. Then they might hit the town afterwards to celebrate—or commiserate. Or both. But of course it wouldn't be right, flaunting her fortune while others stayed back. "Huh," Art said after a lengthy silence, "thought as much."

Maggie hung up the receiver feeling rather off. Her shoes catapulted to the nearest corner and she flopped onto her bed, anger stabbing at her heart. Dora had been downright hostile to her ascendancy—and Harriet's response had been muted to say the least.

She stared at her discarded shoes, pulled the sheet to her chin and shut off the lamp. "Good luck to you," she muttered. After all, she had nothing against their endeavors whatever. She only wished there were more understanding for her singular situation in return, the battle she was waging and well on the way to winning—forging ahead in the name of her own sex.

Chapter Seventeen

She yawned, shaking herself awake and springing from bed, relieved and pleased with her ingenuity. Her plan had worked perfectly. Ted would be proud of her, she mused before swiftly shucking the thought off, annoyed to find him on her mind at so early an hour.

Not a chance, she muttered, admiring the contraption strung from the bedhead. There wasn't a hope in hell of sleeping through the alarm now, not with the thing dangling a few inches shy of her ear, suspended by a ragged strip of material torn from an old dress. Although she did feel a little guilty at having ruined a perfectly wearable dress, after all, it was miles better than ones Harriet made do with.

After nearly a month in Room A3 as Harley Studio's newest in-betweener, Maggie's skills had much improved, but the tricky business of three-quarter profiles was still testing her limits. She took the sketch to John's desk for approval, thrusting it under his nose. By now accustomed to her straightforward ways, John didn't flinch.

"A little more roundness here," he advised, indicating the left cheek of the pipe-smoking fellow in the striped shirt, a newcomer to the Harley stables they hoped would cause a stir among boys, what with Moogle McDoogle's love of adventure, tobacco and fist-fighting.

"More cheek, I see." Maggie tugged the paper from her tutor's hand, "right away." It would take some time before her skills matched the level of her colleagues, but diligence and time would see her fly far beyond expectations—especially as they seemed to be so low where she was concerned.

She returned to her desk, the smallest in the room and half-obscured by a set of bulky shelves. The privacy wasn't so bad. After all, she only need lean back to make herself heard, even if most of what she said was met with icy silence, as though she'd arrived from another planet with no grasp of the native language.

And for all the advantages of her new surrounds, the fashion-able armchairs and matching side-tables arranged in a sociable cluster at the back of the room, the enormous coffee percolator and cookie-tin bursting with sugary goodness, the gramophone and stack of records she hadn't yet heard, Maggie felt her role of interloper most keenly.

If only she had a buddy to share the occasional joke or snide comment with. If only Art hadn't been shown the door just as she'd sailed through another. He would at least have something to say for himself, because John sure as hell didn't—other than providing information about supplies or issuing directions to the ladies' restroom, the nearest being a brisk three-minute walk away.

"So that's how it's done," Maggie said as Ivan stopped the moviola and went about tracing the elephant's outline. It was no wonder Harley critters were so life-like—their walking, running and jumping came directly from real-life footage, not from the imagination of great men. Maggie scowled, recalling John's uncanny bird in the viewing room and feeling a little deceived by it all, "but surely that's cheating…?"

"Milt's secret ingredient, best keep it under your hat, know what I'm saying?" Ivan said as he cranked the loping elephant to the next frame.

A while later Maggie took her pencils to the industrial sharpener in the center of the room. The men were gossiping again, laying bets on when the troublemakers would strike. It was certain to be soon. Despite the calling of more lunch-time lectures, pamphlets were being distributed faster than they could be confiscated, and the rumblings were growing louder. "Just a matter of time," Jack said, as always assured of his rightness, "Wednesday, at the latest," he scowled into the distance, "goddamned Communists."

"Unionists," Maggie said, grinding her pencil to a satisfying point in the great machine, "not the same thing." She hoped Jack wouldn't expect her to elaborate on the distinction, but it wasn't likely, Jack had neither the patience nor curiosity for full-bodied explanations, especially when they came from her.

"Communists or not they got no loyalty," he went on. And what's more he was sick to death of them all, and for that very reason no more was to be said on the subject, except to say the whole business was a very sorry one indeed.

"The Paint and Inkers get peanuts you know," Maggie ventured, her argument somewhat diminished by the grinding of lead...it was a miracle really, how Harriet and Walter both managed to survive on one meagre wage.

"What's wrong with peanuts?" Jack joked, his voice raised above the din, "very tasty." He smacked his lips, basking in his colleagues' amusement.

"Barely enough to live on," Maggie continued, pushing away thoughts of the ruined dress and promising herself she'd make more of an effort, see how Harriet had been getting on lately.

"Where's Milton got to anyways?" Maggie asked Ivan. Of all Milt's men he'd been the most congenial, the most willing to accept her as one of the gang. He shrugged. For the past week not a soul had seen the older Harley brother, and as for the younger one, he never seemed to be available at all, especially not on the couple of occasions Maggie had made a detour to his office on the way back from the restroom.

"My bet's on the Cote d'Azur," Maggie said, giving Jack the side-eye as she retuned to her lair.

"I'll put a fiver on the Riviera," Ivan countered. After all it was the sort of thing Milton did, chartered a plane at a moment's notice, up and left on the turn of a dime.

"But he wouldn't abandon the Orphan at the last hour," Maggie argued. She'd even taken the step of calling Clara to dig up information, had left a message with a grumpy George for the lady of the house to telephone back as soon as possible.

"He'll be back," Ivan assured her.

"But when?" Maggie grumbled, anxious to be granted the pleasure of finally seeing Squirrel Lilly in action. It wasn't too much to ask, *surely*. Maggie looked up, shaken from her reverie by the swinging door.

"It's the old lady," Jack said in a loud whisper. "Adelita—what a pleasant surprise." Maggie froze, her ears as sharp as her newly-ground tools. She leaned back stealthily in her chair and peered out. "To what do we owe the pleasure?" Jack asked.

"No pleasure. I come for Art, he stuff." She strode over to his old desk, now occupied by the terse and humorless John.

"What stuff? He leave a grenade or something?" Jack rose from his desk and stood beside her, "boy what a chump, lets his missus do the dirty work—where is the fella? Stirring up trouble I bet."

"He home," Adelita glared at Jack as John handed her a box. Maggie, still flustered by the surprise visit, held her breath. *Home?*

"Nice dress," Jack said, giving Adelita the once-over and expelling air from his cheeks. She shot him a withering look as he went on, "be sure and say hi to the little fella for us won't you?"

"He so messy," Adelita's dark brows drew together as she inspected the contents of the box.

"Look out," Jack said, "the old man's in trouble now."

"No, he no trouble. You greedy boss man—*he* in trouble."

"Now wait just a minute—" Jack snarled, affronted by her audacity.

"He think he big, big man but we make him pay," she narrowed her eyes, her gaze razor-sharp. Maggie, glad to be a spectator in the matter, retreated further into her burrow. "You no help your friend."

"He's no friend of mine," Jack assured her.

"Yes, you coward. You *all* coward."

Adelita marched from the room, and as Jack leaned from the doorway to supervise her exit, Maggie's anger surged, not just on account of Jack but on account of Art as well. Her fears, it seemed, had been well and truly confirmed, or she reasoned, her suspicions at least. If Art and Adelita had ever been off, they were certainly on now.

"Boy, wouldn't want that coming at me," Jack said after he'd had his fill of ogling, "but wouldn't mind it on me." He sniggered nastily and Maggie, fire rising in her belly, emerged from her enclosure.

"What's that supposed to mean?" she demanded, perfectly aware of his meaning.

"Oops," Jack mugged, retreating to the coffee-station and making a show of tiptoeing away from danger. He thumbed at Maggie as he passed by, "forgot about that one."

"For goodness sake, why do you men pretend to be afraid of us?" Maggie burst out, her heart beating fast, "or *are* you afraid of us?"

"When you're built like Adelita, *sure* I am," Jack sniggered as he filled his mug with over-stewed brew.

Chapter Eighteen

"Tie her up will you?" Ted handed the lead to the zookeeper and Maggie smiled, recognizing the familiar jangling of coins. A bud of warmth bloomed in her belly as he lingered, petting the animal before spotting her among the students. "Look at her coat," Maggie said, turning to Ivan, her nearest neighbor in the semi-circle of easels.

She kept one eye fixed on the deer's dappled haunches and the other on Ted, now feeding a carrot to the long-legged beast—there were apples and hay on the menu as well, but carrots seemed to hold the most sway. She hoped Ted wouldn't leave without some kind of acknowledgement, a wave or a nod of the head…of course *she* could look up and make the first move, but instead she turned to Ivan again, "a lovely pattern, just adorable…"

Their weekly anatomy lessons were held in a studio specially equipped for animal accidents, the trail of neat droppings the adorable deer was currently depositing on the floor without a trace of embarrassment. "Heavens," Maggie smirked as it continued its munching and expelling, "poor thing hasn't any privacy, all of us gawping."

She glanced at Ted and caught him doing the same. He

nodded, awkwardly, but not coldly. There was even a hint of a smile, tentative, but hopeful. A flutter stirred in her breast and she returned her attention to their teacher's instructions. "Observe, observe, observe," he said, pausing briefly as he passed behind each of his pupils to inspect their work. They were to examine the deer's every move, every twitch of muscle, every deer-specific extension of limb and joint.

As she swept her charcoal across the page, pulling her chin to her neck to appraise the lively line, she cast a furtive look at Ted, now petting the deer's ears. And, by the time she reached the bulky muscle at the top of the deer's hind leg she heard foot-steps…and the sweet jingling of coins.

"I did a little of this at Cooper Union, but only boring humans I'm afraid." She glanced over her shoulder, self-conscious and aware of her blushing, "thought you weren't the artistic type?"

"I've a liking for deers."

"I'd say it's rather impossible not to, she's adorable…and squirrels? You like them of course."

"Now that depends on the squirrel. Couple of good ones I know of." He grinned then nodded at the hungry subject, now done with the carrot and making do with the less palatable hay, nudging it with its delicate, black nose, "seems happy enough."

"And not much bothered by all the attention—she's doing a grand job of standing still. Well done girl, very helpful."

"Soft ears," Ted said, his voice full of wonder.

"Are they?"

"Uh-huh. Soft." He straightened and brushed a hand across his mouth, "well, guess I'll see you round?…Least I hope so."

"Yes," her heart filled with joy, "you will."

She waited expectantly, searching his face and detecting a twitch at the top of his jaw. It wasn't quite a solid invitation, but an encouraging start, Maggie decided, suddenly aware of her own cheek-munching, the raw spot only just healed from her last unconscious attack. Ted looked down, his pockets jingling frantically, "the movies then?" he managed, recovering his courage, his eyes reflecting an indoor-gray instead of an outdoor-blue.

"The movies," she agreed, adding a final hint of nostril to the deer's muzzle, "your pick."

"Sure, okay."

"Time's up—" the instructor called out.

"Saturday okay?" Ted cocked his head and Maggie nodded, smiling warmly before returning to the soft-eared deer.

Saturday came and she took his outstretched hand and stepped from the car, taking in the fast-growing metropolis below, the grid of streets and pockets of tall buildings, and, in the distance—but not terribly visible—the Pacific ocean. "You smell like oranges," she said.

"Do I?"

"You do. Lovely. Very fresh."

"A special cologne." Ted scooped a pile of orange-peel from the back seat and searched for a trash-can.

"Over there," Maggie said, adjusting her new hat, one she hoped wasn't too silly. He deposited the peel and returned to her side.

"I sure ate a lot of them in my time."

"Oh? You did?"

"Least two a day. Sometimes more."

"My that *is* a lot."

He'd asked if they might change plans. From a matinee at the Palace Theatre to a hike in Griffith Park. It would be easier to talk, he'd reasoned. But whether they might discuss subjects other than oranges and automobiles was as yet uncertain. "There's your clouds," she said, "come just for you."

"Rain," he predicted, leaning forward in a determined

manner, his spider-like arms swinging at his side as they made off to the three domes and winged bulk of the observatory.

"Should've come prepared," Maggie said, gazing at the precipitous sky, "an umbrella or something." He shot her a concerned look. "Why it's only a little water," she laughed, "it'll wash the dust off."

A drop fell on her cheek, cold and heavy, then another on her arm, then one more on her nose. "Feels rather wonderful…a message from the skies—in morse code." She shut her eyes and reported the coordinates of the landing-spots, "nose…forehead… forehead…cheek…elbow…hat—" When she opened her eyes she saw Ted with his palms turned skyward and eyes shut, his face twitching gently with each drop.

"Come on—" She linked her arm through his and they fell into step, "I wonder what we'll observe," she said in a playful tone. He seemed a little flustered, a little taken-aback by her sudden closeness, and he really did smell lovely, not just of oranges, but of soap and fresh vigor. "Machines I suppose, tele-scopes and the like?"

"You don't mind?" He frowned.

"Not at all," she squeezed his arm companionably and they entered Griffith Observatory.

There were machines. And strange contraptions requiring explanations. She leaned over to examine the giant, bronze ball hovering in the pit below, the impressive pendulum suspended in the center of the atrium, "what's all this about?" Having failed to grasp the significance of the contraption, she followed the barrier round to the explana-tory plaque. "…Foucault pendulum, thirty foot diameter model—"

"How the world rotates," Ted said.

"Oh? How so?"

"Let's see," he began, shifting out the way of two children barreling past like trains broken free from tracks, "…not so sure."

They exchanged smiles and laughed. "Say, they got shows in the planetarium, you ever see one?" He cleared his throat.

"Can't say I have," Maggie said, distracted by the spectacle taking place to her right, the nuzzling couple oblivious to the intensity of their display, "but now we're here."

"Let's see, we got *The Moon, Our Nearest Neighbor* at one." Ted looked up from the pamphlet he'd picked up on the way in.

"I thought you didn't want to sit in the dark?" Maggie teased, still aware of the amorous couple's too-audible kissing, "lets go outside, the rain's stopped."

Not much more had fallen, save a few drops pocking the dirt like tiny craters. "Like the moon," Maggie observed.

"Sure," Ted grinned, "the cheesy moon."

They gazed up at the rocket-like monolith pointing to the heavens. "Astronomers Monument," Ted announced as they examined the stylized figures housed in niches, the celebrated astronomers ringing the base in solemn communion, heroes of past civilizations, bearded and beardless men with stern, wise faces. "Hipparchus, Copernicus, Galileo, Kepler, Newton, Herschel," Ted called out from the other side of the monument.

"You sure know your astronomers," Maggie said, squinting up at one of the more ancient, bearded ones.

"Well," Ted said as he appeared at her side, "I can read anyways."

"Glad to hear it," Maggie laughed as she took over the job of reading herself, "1934. A Public Works Art Project…"

"Or as Milt says, another Roosevelt folly."

"Folly? You don't mean The New Deal do you?" Maggie stiffened, "is that what you think too?"

"Well, there's good and there's bad with it…guess I'm kind of in the middle on that one."

"Know how you feel," Maggie said, her thoughts turning to Harriet and the widening rift between them.

"When the war comes there'll be one project and one project

only."

"But Roosevelt says we won't go."

"Huh—you mean we'll sit on the fence."

"It's got nothing to do with fences," Maggie shot back as Ted's hand passed over the smooth, white stone, "oh let's not talk about the war."

Truth be told, Harriet had similar doubts about their president's promise to stay out of any conflict. War was good for business apparently. "Say, wanna see my secret place?" Maggie tugged Ted in the direction of the car, "my little river?"

"Sure."

"Run!" Maggie called out, encouraging Ted to match her cracking pace down the trail to the tiny, woodland stream. She stopped, waiting for him to catch up, shielding her eyes as she gazed at the sky, the clouds dissolving into cotton-candy wisps under the heat of the giant sun. "Will you go?" Maggie asked when he'd reached her side, suddenly breaking her rule of not talking about the war, "if there is one?"

"I'll pitch in," he held her gaze steadily, "if it comes to that."

"Yes," she said, grateful for the amendment, "if it comes to that. Here, this is it—where Lilly started her adventure." She settled onto the stone-age chair, "and here's her leaf—or boat I should say," she plucked a vessel from the nearest hanging fleet, "not the same one of course, but one just like it. Its brother perhaps. Here—go ahead and launch her."

Ted placed the vessel in the water and Maggie saluted to the imaginary passenger about to set sail, "tally-ho…bon voyage."

"Tally-ho?"

"Tally-ho—terribly useful for galloping about shooting foxes. My father was posted in London for a time."

"You shoot any foxes?"

"Good heavens no, I shouldn't like that at all."

The vessel bobbed and rocked in the trickle's flow, its path unimpeded by turtle-rocks or menacing twigs. "How you getting along in A3?" Ted nudged the boat away from a stagnant eddy and it surged onward with renewed momentum, "Maggie the animator."

"Maggie the animator," she repeated, beaming, "she's getting along just fine. Except for Jack."

"Jack's an ass."

"Yes I rather think he is. But Milt says Lilly's got potential and I'm inclined to agree, oh isn't it terrific—he wasn't a bit mad about it—of course the story needs work, a little oiling here and there."

"She sure is a charmer."

"Only thing is I won't know *how* charming you see…until I *see* her." She let out a great sigh and stole a look at the boss's little brother, "I wonder if…well, if you might ask—has he said anything about a meeting? To go over the particulars?"

"Nope," Ted dunked his hand in the stream and swirled it about, "not my area I'm afraid." The boat suddenly flipped, it's journey cut short by an unexpected beaching.

"Shoot. Didn't quite make it." Maggie plucked another vessel and launched it into the stream, "where's he got to anyways? Skipped town has he? Taking a break from the communists." The boat bobbed and surged in the miniature river, twisting and turning in frantic circles, "and firing Art won't solve anything— only make things worse. Beats me why the two of them can't put an end to the nonsense and come to an understanding, then we can all get on with things."

"Not as straightforward as you think," Ted said, regarding her a little cooly, "things are a little tight right now."

"Tight?" Maggie snorted, folded her arms and raised her brows, "I should say if anyone's getting the squeeze it's us—well, folks like Harriet I mean…poor Hattie. Anyways—if Harley can afford a forty-thousand dollar camera…well, I rest my case."

"Twenty-eight thousand five hundred and ninety-five dollars," Ted said, setting the story straight, "thought you said you don't believe everything you read?"

"Of course not."

She snatched up a stick and dug in the dirt, chasing away thoughts of the pamphlet she'd helped create. By now every single Harley employee had seen it. She looked up at Ted, perched on a rock, his lanky legs on either side with knees pointing up and out like a grasshopper. He tossed a pebble and it skimmed across the surface before sinking to the bottom. "Bravo," she said softly. There was silence, then the sound of crunching pebbles as Ted searched for another stone. "Art's the best animator we've got," she ventured finally, "*had*—I should say."

"Not according to Milt," Ted shrugged and tossed another stone.

"Oh, so it's jealousy is it?"

"Milton or Schrieber?"

"Well..."

"More alike than they care to admit—both hot-heads for starters."

They sat for a while, silent save for the trickle of water and birds squawking overhead, catapulting from branch to branch in the shady canopy. "So? Where is he then? We're all terribly curious. Taking bets as a matter of fact, odds are on the Riviera." She tossed the stick over her shoulder and winked, "care to slip me a little inside information?"

"He's been ill..." Ted stood abruptly, his face suddenly swamped by worry. The jangling started up and Maggie swallowed.

"Oh dear, has he...?"

"Just a cold gone to his chest is all...be back on his feet in no time."

"Good, yes—I'm sure he'll be right as rain soon enough."

· · ·

They arrived back at Ted's car and Maggie caught sight of a bright patch of color. She pointed to the sack of oranges peeking out from behind the front seat, "got one for me?" He hesitated, then rummaged about to find the best one. "You must be awfully fond of them," Maggie teased as she dug her finger into the fragrant skin, "two a day and all."

"Folks are in the business," he explained, smiling fondly, "get a big ole sack every week."

"All that vitamin C, you'll live to a ripe old age."

"Here—" He took the orange and stripped the skin in a blink of an eye, and, after splitting the fruit in two, pushed a segment free with his thumb, "sweetest you'll get."

"Why I never saw a thing like it," Maggie exclaimed, astonished by the feat, "was that magic?"

"Nope," he smiled, pleased with the trick, "nine seconds is my best—Milt's is ten, might be the only thing where I had him beat."

"That so?" Maggie sprang sideways to avoid spurting juice. She licked a trail of sweet liquid from her hand, "well I don't believe it for a second. Bet Milton can't fix a sick automobile or a drawer—or a camera for that matter."

"Nope, you're right there," he opened the passenger door, "guess we oughta make tracks…getting kind of late."

"Oh no we can't waste a good sunset," she said, heading to a bench overlooking the valley, "and I have it on good authority *this* one is terrific." She motioned for him to sit, "hurry now, the eight o'clock session is about to start—oh isn't it funny, how we ended up right where we started?"

It was inevitable, she explained as he sat by her side, they'd wound up at the movies after all, found their very own picture-theatre showing the most panoramic movie of all, the great outdoors, the glorious orange valleys dotted with nests of gray-blue sage. "Popcorn?" She passed an imaginary bucket and sipped on an imaginary straw.

"Don't mind if I do," he said, grinning from ear to ear at her antics. She leaned back, sated from the orange and her make-believe refreshments.

"So what's it's like? Growing up on a farm?"

"Orange grove."

"Pardon me—orange grove." She turned, taking in the line of his profile in the soft, pillowy light, the slight curve of his nose, the Adam's apple jutting out like ancient canyon rock, "all that picking and planting and hoeing and I'm sure I don't know what else."

"We were poor—for the most part." His arm brushed hers, and as he shifted in his seat he stole a glance at his companion, "every kid in the neighborhood ran wild, me and Milt included."

"And it's nothing to be ashamed of—"

"Who said anything about being ashamed?"

"No of course not—I didn't mean that," Maggie colored, "and now you live in a great big house in the Hollywood Hills, a terrific success."

"That's right, Mountfield Gates."

"Maids and chauffeurs, cocktails and fancy automobiles…and girls too I suppose."

"Oh plenty of girls."

She leaned into his shoulder and right on cue he slung his arm around the back of the seat. She felt the warmth of his arm radiate to the back of her neck, the hairs on her arm prickle. Her eyes roamed over the valley below as she willed him to turn to her and kiss her in the soft, enveloping light.

"Hey–!" Maggie shouted, flapping her hands to disperse the cloud of dust kicked up by a departing car, "why how do you like *that* for manners?" She waved a fist at the offending vehicle as it careened off down the road. Her heart sunk. The delicate moment, she realized, was well and truly over.

Chapter Nineteen

She scooted her chair back to get a better view. At last
Milton had resurfaced. Now she might finally get her
chance. "Party's at Ed's, not mine," the boss informed his top
men. They were all invited, even the one with the lovely legs
residing behind the shelf.

"Better pool there," Jack noted, the remark setting off a
knowing chuckle among the men of A3.

"Still up to the back-teeth in rubble," Milton said of his own
abode, currently filled with masons, carpenters and painters
scrambling to finish the overdue works, improvements that had
dragged on for more than a year.

"Time to schmooze huh?" John said, "guess someone's gotta
do it."

"Afraid so," Milton agreed of the obligatory shindig thrown to
whip up publicity for *The Little Orphan*. As well as access to Ted's
seemingly notorious pool, guests would be treated to all manner
of exotic cocktails and edibles. And to top things off, the songbird
herself would sing—the very same canary who'd warbled the
night away at The Blue Note. "See you fellas tonight." Milton
raised his hand in farewell and turned to leave.

"Hold up—" Maggie called out, catapulting from her seat before the boss managed his escape.

"What is it?" Milton shot her a warning look, "what's on your mind?" he added, less gruffly.

"My squirrel." Maggie steeled herself for a possible onslaught, "the meeting you promised—I'm terribly eager to hear your thoughts, and *see* her, see my cartoon."

"Meeting?"

"Yes meeting…"

"I don't recall making any promises."

Maggie, drawing herself up to full height—and suppressing a strong urge to aim a swift kick at his shin—spoke slowly and evenly, "to talk the story over…you said she needs work, that's what you said."

"Yes yes, so I did. We'll talk about it later."

"Yes, but when?" Maggie pressed, noting his pallid color. Up close he didn't look so good, older and grayer somehow, his skin a little papery.

"Soon. After the premiere."

"Swell," Maggie exhaled, somewhat satisfied with the answer, "oh I just know the Orphan will be a terrific hit."

"Let's hope so…still, I know a shortcut to the river if she tanks," he forced a weary smile, "now back to work."

"We're all rooting for her," Maggie lied as the door closed behind him.

It wasn't true. Neither Harriet nor Art nor any of the union 'thugs' cared a whit about the goddamned Orphan's debut on the big screen. All they cared about was getting the numbers to strike and throwing a big fat spanner right into the heart of Milt's publicity machine. The bigger the better.

The afternoon dragged on. Yet more iterations of Moogle McDoogle and his incessant pipe-smoking. Recent episodes had taken a military turn with the wearing of navy blues complete with neckerchief and dixie-cup hat. She turned to Ivan to voice her concerns. "Surely smoking isn't allowed in submarines. Can't be safe."

"Oh but anything can happen in the land of Harley."

"A land of miracles," Maggie said, her tone reminiscent of Harriet's sardonic drawl.

Weeks had passed since their last encounter, an accidental one, passing like ships in the night, each hurrying to their respective Harley stations. She wondered if she and Harriet were still friends at all, or if their differences were too great to mend. "Silly fellow," Maggie muttered, scowling at the chain-smoking sailor as she listened to the men gossip.

"Spends all day down at Morley Hall," Jack informed the room, "least what I heard."

"Yeah?"

"Milt's got a man down there keeping an eye on things."

"Hey—" John hissed at Jack, "zip it will ya?" Maggie held her breath, her ears flapping as the men went on.

"She's all right," Ivan said in a low tone.

"Glad you think so," Maggie quipped, emerging from her lair and heading to the coffee station. Ivan shot her an apologetic look.

"Get me one will you?" Jack ordered as Maggie emptied the last of the coffee into her mug, "you don't mind topping it up do you?"

"Not at all," Maggie said through gritted teeth.

"You coming tonight?" Ivan asked her.

"Wouldn't miss it for the world," Maggie said as she wrenched a filter from the box and stuffed it in the percolator.

"Sure you're invited?" Jack sniggered.

"*Very*, but then I guess Milt mightn't have seen me behind the barricade and all," Maggie said as she supervised the liquid's slow drip. As a matter of fact her attendance at the party had been decided two days prior via a telephone call from Clara, bored with her lounging and searching for a friend to keep her company. The matter had been promptly settled. Maggie would be Clara's particular guest, to save her from the likes of John's wife and the man with the clammy hands.

"Yeah yeah—keep your hat on," Jack said, vowing to make good on his promise. Just as soon as they found another spot for the obfuscating shelf, the thing would be moved.

"It's in your interests," Maggie argued. If she were more visible then perhaps they'd be less inclined to make disrespectful comments with regard to certain parts of a lady's anatomy—Adelita's visit still lingered in Jack's mind apparently, not so much the content, but the form of it.

"Here," Jack pushed his mug to the edge of his desk for Maggie's greater convenience.

"Jack. You don't mind fixing your own, do you?" She ignored the mug and returned to her desk, buoyed by her small act of rebellion. He scowled and sulked as she passed by. "Matter of fact let's make a rule of it shall we? Each of us responsible for our own drinks? That strike you as fair?"

"Okay with me," Ivan said without looking up.

"Fair?" Jack snorted. He shook his head and continued his mumblings, "that's fine talk coming from you."

Maggie's face burned. It wasn't the first time Jack had cast aspersions her way…her 'convenient' friendship with Ted, the promotion that had somehow fallen from the sky into her very 'lucky' lap. She ground her pencil into the paper, not caring if Moogle McDoogle's eyes were a little skewed. Jack was utterly wrong. It wasn't like that at all, not a whit. Ted had provided a leg up with a key to a room, that was all, the hard work had been all hers.

"Gotta hand it to Milt," Jack said to no one in particular—or to Maggie more particularly, "guess it's a kind of insurance poli-cy." He swept up his mug, and heading off to fix his own drink, explained his reasoning. If the country went to war it would certainly need airplanes and tanks and guns, but it would still need animators, and if girls were the only option, then girls would have to do.

As Jack kept up his yammering, Maggie set Moogle McDoogle aside and sketched the picture forming in her mind, a great, big hammer crashing down on Jack's smug head, his body ramming into the ground like a steel girder. Satisfied with the caricature she propped it on her desk for general display—if anyone cared to visit, that was. She tipped her chair back and glared at Jack, hoping to bring on one of his headaches with the power of her mind.

Chapter Twenty

Ted Harley's house was as much a mansion up close as it was from afar, its white Mediterranean grandeur rising from the greenery in multi-level splendor. Colored lanterns illuminated well-tended hedgerows and palm trees reached for the sky, their trunks wound with spirals of lights. Maggie turned the wheel and drove through the iron gates flanked by gloved men in box-hats and toy soldier uniforms, attending to their duty with just the right amount of friendliness and pomp.

Clara ran towards her across the vast patio. It had taken quite a time for Maggie to reach the pool area out back, the private playground of Mr Edward Harley. Ferns bowed in the breeze, their green dulled to black in the light of night. "Well will you look at you," Clara said before letting out an approving whistle, "scrub up pretty good, dontcha?" She swiped two drinks from a fast moving tray, "hey! Slow down will ya?" She glared, wiping spilt liquid from her arm as the scantily-clad waitress hurried away. "Geez, that really burns me up—silly nogoodnik," she yelled out. The waitress turned.

"Look'n right at ya," she shouted back. Clara laughed and Maggie, astonished at the frank exchange, frowned.

"Oh we go way back, busting our chops at Paramount—she's certifiable," Clara added, as though aspiring to the same state.

"An actress?"

"Wannabe, more like."

Clara's own efforts at screen success had been similarly short-lived, but in the end it hadn't mattered anyhow. Evidently, during the process of busting her chops she'd been lucky enough to meet Milton at a Hollywood party, and that, as they say, was that. She elbowed Maggie, identifying the screen-dream faces and infinitely less attractive industry bigwigs—not to mention any major or minor scandals they may or may not have committed. "Well? Don't just stand there like a stuffed duck—" she shoved a champagne at Maggie, "stop your goofing and start boozing will ya?"

"Where's the boss?" Maggie took the delicate glass and sipped soberly.

"Beats me," Clara shrugged, doing her best to appear casual, "he'll be around."

Maggie felt the breeze on her shoulders, glad of her latest purchase. Although flimsy, and with a great propensity to ripple fetchingly in the breeze, the pale-blue satin dress had quite enough material to cover the entirety of her back. "There's your butter and eggs man," Clara pointed to the stage, complete with velvet backdrop and crown of dancing neon notes, "guess he's not so bad."

Maggie watched as Ted wrangled with a drum, fixing it to its frame with steady patience. He motioned to a nearby band member and they wrestled with the instrument together. "Not bad from this angle," Clara said, her eyes narrowing as she appraised Ted's assets. She pinched Maggie's rear.

"Oh get away with you!" Maggie said, slapping her away, "I suppose he *is* rather handsome don't you think? Not much of a talker—"

"No kidding, the guy's catatonic." Clara's brow shot up at

Maggie's surprise, "what you gawping at? You ain't the only one with fancy words."

"Of course not, no…Ted's just a little shy is all."

"Yeah yeah all I'm saying is get your hooks in and be quick about it—else I'm gonna puke."

Soon enough the party got into full swing, long-legged beauties and even-featured men doing their best to keep step with one another as the songbird swooped and soared. Maggie, suddenly feeling a little catatonic herself, took shelter in the shadow of a palm, watching on as Ted chatted with a man in an old-fashioned derby hat.

"Coming through…make way," Maggie said finally, emerging from the shadows and weaving her way between a harried-looking waitress and three men in the throes of hysterical laughter. She spotted the derby and adjusted her course, but by the time she arrived, Ted had gone.

"Where's Ted?" she asked the man with the hat.

"Ed? Couldn't rightly say," he leaned in to her ear, grinning, "but if he's got an ounce of sense he'll come right on back. You his sweetheart? God help him if you're not." She felt a tap on her shoulder and swung round to find Clara fresh from a turn on the dance-floor with the boss, her eyes shining with excitement.

"You bring your bathing-suit?" she asked Maggie, all the while keeping Milton in a firm grip at her side. He panted, his chest heaving with exertion.

"Afraid not."

"No matter, we got spares—Ed got spares, baby?" she turned to Milton with the question.

"Sure," he waved a hand at the house, "go ask inside."

"Hello Mr Harley…"

"Hello Maggie."

"He got towels too?" Clara said.

"Course he got towels!" Milton exploded.

"Geez! What you so evil about?" Clara brushed imaginary dust from his shoulder and he leaned over to whisper in her ear.

"Okay baby," Clara smiled, "but gimmie a little honey-cooler first," she pressed a finger to her lips and he complied with a quick kiss. "*Business*," Clara shuddered, her stiff, platinum waves showing no sign of losing their footing, "I'll take a dip but I gotta watch the mop." She struck a hackneyed pose and patted her hair, "so, you like?"

Everything had been taken care of, dress, face, hair. The whole palaver, Clara revealed, had been nothing but a blast. And she hadn't felt the slightest bit bored all day. "I got plenty to do," she said, keeping an eye on Milton as he left, her pretty shoulders slumping, "guess he's still a little peaky."

"Just a cold gone to his chest I suspect," Maggie placed her glass on the railing with excessive care, "it isn't as bad as all that."

"Course it ain't," Clara scowled.

They went in search of bathing-suits, available in the change-room set aside for the ladies' convenience. "Good heavens—" Maggie stopped dead in her tracks, her jaw dangling in awe—if there'd been a train nearby it could have driven right through. "No..." she intoned, her eyes wide with disbelief, "it *can't* be...is that...?"

"Upstairs. Second room on the right," Clara said, repeating the instructions she'd just received from a helpful toy-soldier.

"Is it? *No...*" Maggie stood motionless, rooted to the ground as Clara yanked her arm.

"Who? Clark Gable?" Clara said, pivoting her head in the direction of Maggie's open-mouthed gaze. "Oh—" she said, disappointed, "that James Cagney fella huh?"

Maggie all at once felt weak, light-headed, as though her legs might form a puddle beneath her if she wasn't careful. "Well don't just stand there like a stuffed duck," Clara sighed, "go say how de do. You got three seconds. One...two—"

"Yes alright—seize the day and all that." But as Maggie

steeled herself for the momentous occasion the man turned and revealed himself to be an equally handsome but infinitely less interesting person. Maggie, laughing at her mistake, ran up the stairs close on Clara's tail.

They locked the door of the change-room and rifled through the basket of brand new bathing-suits, Maggie extracting a black number with a fine, white belt. "Let's have a look-see," Clara said as she knotted her own discovery, a daring halterneck with a plunging neck-line.

Maggie emerged from behind the screen, checking her reflection in the full-length mirror. She hadn't planned on taking a dip, but as Clara pointed out, Ted's pool was not only too good to be true but too good to waste. "There. Ready for the plunge," Maggie said, slipping her fingers under the leg-holes and stretching the suit to cover more skin.

"Boy is Ed gonna flip."

"Really, Clara," Maggie chided, as though the thought would never cross her mind when in fact it already had.

Clara screamed out as she lost balance and crashed into the water. Maggie hadn't been able to resist the temptation, besides, it was the only way to shut her up about Ted, who disappointingly was still nowhere to be seen. She grinned wickedly as Clara thrashed her way back to safety and clung to the side of the pool, her face streaked with clown-like mascara. "Why the hell d'ya do that?"

"Oh I just felt like it," Maggie breezed as she searched the crowd for her gentle octopus...perhaps he'd been called away to urgent business, the type requiring a dark room, a bottle of whiskey and the exclusive company of men. But the picture didn't fit...Ted with a cigar moored in the corner of his mouth. *No*, Maggie mused as she dipped a hand in the gently lapping water, Ted looked far better with a toolbox or a spanner, or leaning over her lap explaining the ins and outs of the Pussycat...

"It ain't funny," Clara sulked.

"Sorry—here, fix your face." Maggie tossed Clara a towel and went in search of another peace token, a coconut-rum concoction that according to another of the wannabe actresses was the bee's knees and no two ways about it.

"Okay, okay—!" Maggie sprang back as Clara rose like Neptune from the deep and latched onto her arm. There was no choice about getting wet now, the platinum sea-goddess wouldn't let up, not now her hair had been so thoroughly ruined. "Here goes nothing," Maggie said, shaking free and diving right in.

The water was just the right kind of warm. She spread her limbs like a starfish, the music muffling as her ears dipped below the surface. She gazed at the black sky, the speckle of heavenly bodies made of cheese or some kind of supersonic rock…Ted would take her back to the observatory and they could discover the universe together…Mars and Jupiter and Neptune and the billions of stars that might forever remain unknown. Water lapped at her forehead as she scooped her hands like fins, her body rotating like a canoe changing tack. "Watch out!" Clara yelled, pushing Maggie's long legs out the way, "where's Milt anyways?" she pouted, shivering like a drowned rat.

They got out, dried off, and after a few false leads found Clara's man taking a break from the hullabaloo in a dark room. Or perhaps not so dark—*some* light was required to find the whiskey bottle and decipher aces from jacks and kings. "Makes everyone play," Clara said, opening the door to the library and poking her head in without fear of reprisal. Maggie scanned the occupants. Milton, John, Jack and several other bigwigs playing a smoky game of poker.

"What you boys up to?" Clara purred. She'd donned a flouncy garment over her bathing-suit, though it couldn't have been for modesty's sake, the sheerness of the material created quite the opposite effect.

"Don't forget to ask about my film—you won't forget will you?"

"I said I'd work on him didn't I?" Clara hissed over her shoulder, half-closing the door in Maggie's face.

"It's only I'm rather getting to the end of my rope—" Maggie managed before the door shut with a decisive click.

She left Clara to poker and the comfort of Milton's lap, somewhat satisfied she would do her bidding when the time was right, find out what *soon* meant in Milton's particular dictionary.

She hurried back to the pool, eager to commune with the water again, continue her blissful, buoyant imaginings…a starfish, a jellyfish, a shark, a canoe…a giant stand of seaweed—all the while hoping she'd emerge from her watery paradise and find Ted mesmerized by her aquatic performance.

"Excuse me—which way to the change-room?" A good hour later she pushed past men and women languishing against walls and doors and any available surface in the crowded hallway, "where the blazes is it?" she muttered, aware of the many eyes appraising her form. She tightened the towel about her waist, retracing the route in her mind and figuring she must've taken a bum turn.

As two men approached, lurching and cackling, Maggie squeezed into a corner. "Give it here," one of them said, snatching his companion's cigarette and lumbering past in a smoky haze. Maggie, having already checked three of the rooms along the seemingly endless hallway, turned the next handle. She heard music from within, a horn or trumpet or some such thing.

"*There* you are," she exclaimed. Ted turned, his eyes wide at the glorious sight before him. "I must say you've terrific taste in bathing-suits," she grinned, her cheeks rosy from calisthenics and the restorative qualities of coconut and rum. She let go the towel and gave him an eyeful, then, a little surprised by her mini striptease, repackaged herself in the scanty apparel. "My fingers are like sea-cucumbers," she said, going over to show off her puckered skin, "aren't they odd? I wonder if mermaids have the same problem? I didn't want to get out at all but I had to find you—have you been hiding here all night?"

"Not hiding, I–ah…" he put the brass instrument down.

"Oh, hallo there," Maggie said, suddenly aware of a diminutive man cradled in a large sofa-chair, one of the band members she guessed, the drummer perhaps.

"Chuck—this is Maggie." Ted cleared his throat and the older man nodded.

"How do you do."

"How do you do," Maggie said, suddenly terribly self-conscious in her half-naked state.

"I'll leave you two to it." Chuck raised his knees, swung himself out of the great chair and clapped Ted on the back, "keep up the good work now."

"I sure will," Ted said as Chuck paused at the door and let out a particularly tuneful wolf-whistle. He motioned to Maggie as he addressed the host, "one helluva set of pins she got there—oh *yeah*."

"Don't mind him," Ted said when Chuck had gone.

"Oh? Why should I mind?" Maggie crossed her arms, all at once feeling rather too exposed, "the only thing I mind is not knowing the whereabouts of my dress."

"You get lost?"

"As a matter of fact I did." She frowned, then picked up the brass instrument, "so you play this thing huh?"

"Yup, a trumpet."

"Yes I thought as much," she fibbed.

"Careful—" Ted said, rushing to her assistance, his hands hovering less her feminine strength fail. She shot him an exasperated look.

"I'm quite capable of lifting the thing. The trumpet." She pressed the mouthpiece to her lips, "like this?"

"Uh-huh, but you gotta work your cheeks some." He pursed his lips to demonstrate, blowing his face into chipmunk mounds.

But when Maggie did the same, the only music that came from the fluted tube was the sound of her own frustration.

"That can't be right. Show me how it's done."

She handed the trumpet back and he lifted it to his lips, filling it with breath. The result was nothing like her own wheezy, deflating effort, it was clear, strong and with great intention—the tune she didn't recognize, but it was jazz—she knew that much. "You're very good."

"Getting better."

"It's terrific…even if it is jazz," she wandered over to the open window and leaned out, "darn confounding if you ask me."

"Takes a little tuning into is all."

"Oh? Let it flow, is that the trick?" she waved down at Clara, currently the centre of attention in a circle of male admirers.

"I saw you, you know…"

"In the pool?" Maggie turned and leant against the sill, an impish smile on her lips.

"No…at The Blue Note."

"Oh—" Maggie turned away, flustered and embarrassed.

"Thought you were sick in bed? A bad sore throat wasn't it?" She gulped, her head bowed guiltily.

"So hot," she exclaimed, hoping they'd forget about The Blue Note and start afresh, "goodness—it must be ninety out there."

She looked about the room, the walls thoroughly festooned with drums, bells, ukuleles and guitars of all shapes and sizes— short-necked and long, bulbous and flat. "Boy—you got quite the collection here huh? *And* a piano—may I?" She skipped over to the ivory-keyed beauty and took a seat.

"You play?" Ted asked.

"Nuh-uh, not a bit."

"Not even chopsticks?"

"Not even Chopsticks," she pressed a key tentatively then pressed again, "that's a sad one."

He sat beside her, his shoulder brushing hers as he belted out the simple tune, "you know a lady wrote Chopsticks?"

"Huh. Is that a fact."

"Just the tune for starting out. Wanna give it a shot?"

"Sure."

She turned to him eagerly, felt a magnetic pull as their eyes met and his hands splayed over hers, heat radiating as two sets of fingers pressed notes in unison—

"It's Milt—!" John cried, suddenly bursting through the door with great urgency, "had one of his turns."

Ted, on high alert, extricated himself from the piano-stool and followed in John's wake, calling over his shoulder as he left, "change-room's that-a-way, three doors down—"

Chapter Twenty-One

Three hours later Maggie sprang from bed and clambered through the dark. The telephone was ringing out, a clear, insistent bell in the hollow of night. "Yes? Who is it?"

"Mags—I'm in a jam, he won't budge and I…won't you come?" It was Harriet, on the verge of tears and desperate for help.

"I'll come right away."

"When he's at Morley Hall he's fine," Harriet said with a tremulous sigh, "otherwise he's a monster, a big, idiot monster."

"Morley Hall?" Maggie frowned at her sleepy reflection.

"Morley Hall," Harriet said loudly, as though volume might fix her friend's faulty memory, "union headquarters, ring a bell? 1182 Juno Street if you're ever interested," she added, inserting the familiar edge into her voice.

"Now I recall, yes…Morley Hall," Maggie fiddled with the telephone cord, "only I haven't much time…" Her sheepish comment was met with silence.

"Forget it. Can you come or not?"

"Hang tight, I'll be there in a jiffy."

She drove to Bunker Hill at breakneck pace, the empty streets aiding a speedy trip. She might never grace the steps of Morley Hall to do her bit—but as far as rescuing Harriet at four in the morning was concerned, there wasn't a single second thought.

She ran up the steps to the front door. Harriet was waiting, her finger pressed to her lips. "Keep it quiet," she warned. If the superintendent woke there'd be hell to pay, and, Maggie suspected, a substantial sum of back-rent. "This way," Harriet whispered, guiding Maggie around the worst of the creaky floorboards to the back door.

Outside under a bush was the problem at hand. Harriet prodded Walter's leg with her foot. "Wake-up," she hissed, the whites of her eyes visible in the moonlight. She shook his inert body as Maggie stood by, horrified at the sight of a grown man moaning incoherently, his fists balled under his chin like a child afraid of the dark, "move it—" Harriet ordered as she crouched beside him.

The last of Harriet's wage had been sunk into a bottle of whiskey, and after five hours of solid drinking—and enraged by an order to take out the trash—Walter had knocked the coffeepot off the stove and kicked a hole in the wall, not even allowing Harriet to remove his sock to check for a damaged toe. He'd then migrated to his present position, half-asleep in a heap of snoring, defeated flesh.

His wife shook him harder then spoke in a more kindly tone, "let's get you to bed."

"Lee-me alone," he slurred woefully, "lee-me alone…"

"One arm each," Maggie directed as they heaved Walter to a sitting position and dragged him to the porch. He lolled his head in Maggie's direction, his eyes bloodshot, angry and full of shame.

"Lee-me alone," he moaned again as the women hauled him through the door to the foot of the stairs. He let out a determined yowl, shaking the women free and managing an upright position before tripping, his hand missing the rail and slipping between the uprights.

His head met the stairs with a sickening thud. "Walt!" Harriet gasped as Maggie stepped back to give her room. Much to their relief there was no sign of blood, and the impact seemed to have sobered him up somewhat. He felt at his head, rubbing the spot that would soon grow to a nasty lump. "Bed," he mumbled, his protestations finally at an end.

When Walter had been safely interred Harriet offered coffee to her rescuer. "Yes all right," Maggie said, suddenly weak, "is he often like this?" She collapsed in the nearest chair as Harriet heated water on the portable gas-cooker.

"Worse since he got fired. Thing is, when he starts up he can't stop. Like some kind of crazy man." She shook her head sadly.

"It must be terribly upsetting. Putting up with it all." Maggie wrinkled her nose at the unpleasant smell wafting from the chair and rose to fetch a cup, relocating to a less aromatic seat.

"Oh…sorry," Harriet's face fell as she replaced the lid of the cookie-tin, "all gone…still, least it means he ate something." She sat, cradling her mug and retreating into herself, her eyes flat and unseeing as Walter's gargantuan snores rose and fell from his cradle in the corner of the room, the bed pushed to the wall and cordoned off with a makeshift curtain.

"What can I do to help?" Maggie reached across the table to take Harriet's hand.

"He'll be fine once we get him down the picket-line," she emptied the last of her coffee in the sink and turned the mug on end.

"Picket-line," Maggie breathed, her eyes lowered, "but how can *you* afford to go without wages?"

"Can't afford not to is how I look at it. We gotta stand up for what's right."

"Yes, but…"

"But what?"

"Nothing."

"Then you'll join us?" Harriet said, dubious.

"Well I—I'd like to help but you see it's rather difficult—"

"Sure, you got your own business to figure out. Hollywood parties and the like."

Maggie's face burned as they tiptoed down to the front-porch. "Listen, forget it, I didn't mean that…thanks for lending a hand."

"Sure," Maggie said, her voice stiff as she made her way to the street, "anytime, anytime at all."

Chapter Twenty-Two

*S*he barely slept a wink. The few hours between rescuing Walter and rising from bed had been spent tossing and turning, and as she approached the studio lot, slowing the Pussycat to walking pace, she saw her fears had finally been realized.

There must have been a hundred or so Harley employees gathered at the giant barred gates, a hundred or so strikers ready to fight for their rights. "Fair day's pay for a fair day's work—fair day's pay for a fair day's work—fair day's pay for a fair day's work!"

"What's that?" Maggie cupped her ear as she drove alongside her chanting colleagues—if she could make out the slogan she might well belt out a round to show her support, "how's it go?"

"Read the sign, dummy," a man said, shoving a placard in her face.

"Hey—careful with that stick," she warned, her impulse to join in now gone, "make way please—" She spotted Art, his face set in determination, "good luck," she called out as she maneuvered the Pussycat through the writhing mob.

"Enjoy that fence," Art yelled above the ruckus. Maggie

stepped on the brake and the Pussycat came to a sharp halt. "Nice party last night?"

"Now listen here, *I'm* not the enemy—"

"Yeah but you're sleeping with him," came another man's voice. Maggie blanched, turning to her accuser with fury.

"How *dare* you!"

"Hey—quit it," Art said, chastising the offender, who Maggie soon saw was Bert.

"As a matter of fact I'm on your side," she eyed Bert dangerously, "we oughta be paid more, especially the women—matter of fact I plan on having a word to Mr Harley about it when I get the chance…" she trailed off, coloring at her arrogance. Uncle Milt hadn't even the respect to show her the cartoon she'd slaved over for months on end—he would hardly entertain her views on industrial matters, the idea was absurd…

"Fat chance," Bert said with a rueful snort.

"Good luck," Maggie mumbled, a foreboding feeling congealing in her gut, "and I've said I'll help…however I can," she added, appealing to Harriet, now just visible over Art's shoulder, "isn't that right Hattie?"

"Let her be," Harriet said, her voice flat and eyes averted.

"How's Walter holding up—?" Maggie rushed on, desperate for a sign their friendship was still on the mend.

"Move it will you!" A horn beeped from behind, an impatient car held up by Maggie's feeble negotiations. She sounded her own horn, a long, low blast as she passed through the gates, her mouth dry and heart pounding fast.

"What's eating you?" Jack said as Maggie arrived at Room A3. "Where'd that happy-go-lucky girl get to?" She ought to be jubilant, he figured, on account of the the shelf having at last been removed—she was now apparently free of any and all impediments to success.

"We'll see about that," she arranged her tools, took in the improved view and nodded brusquely, "better." But truth be told, she didn't feel any calmer now she'd reached the safety of her desk, in fact, she felt worse—exposed, as though a great wind might blow through her and turn her to dust. She stared at the paper, her pencil poised to be of service to Moogle McDoogle and his stupid military adventures. Her head ached, a pounding in tandem with the anxious beat in her chest.

"You come through the front?" Ivan asked, careful to exclude Jack from the exchange.

"Uh-huh."

"Go round back next time. Delivery gate."

"They got no respect," Jack said loudly, "all Milt's done for us…goddamned Communists—every last one of them."

Maggie looked round at the gang, Milton's coterie of loyal men, their brows pulled into various states of disapproval…on second thoughts she wasn't sure she liked the new view one bit.

"Cup of Joe?" Ivan picked up her mug, "one sugar or two?"

"It needs a wash—oh, and three, please…"

"Think I can manage that." He drummed his fingers on her desk and headed to the sink.

She smiled, grateful for an ally in the hostile environment. But Jack hadn't finished. "Not right in the head," he said to his usual audience of no-one in particular, "so screwed up they can't tell right from wrong."

"They're not Communists," Maggie ventured bravely, "they're unionists and not the least screwed up. They want a fair day's pay for a fair day's work—particularly the women."

"*Particularly the women*," Jack mocked, "we got ourselves a red in the ranks, that's right fellas—a bona-fide sympathizer."

"I'll have you know we—the *women* do a hell of a lot of work down at Paint and Ink."

"Oh yeah? All that coloring-in huh?" Jack let out an incredulous laugh.

Maggie, fuming, returned to Moogle McDoogle's misadventure astride a submarine rocket. The only thing to be done about Jack was ignore him, a task made more difficult now the shelf had been removed. Now she was positively forced to look at the back of his stupid head whenever she came up for air...perhaps she'd request the shelf be reinstated.

She sighed inwardly, glaring at the twenty-odd pages of incorrectly-drawn nose—John always thought *her* best suited to fixing other people's mistakes. She snorted, erasing the bulbous nose aggressively, her mind drifting to more pleasant lands.

Ted. Their shoulders brushing at the piano, his chipmunk cheeks and pursed lips...the stunned look on his undeniably handsome face when she'd dropped her towel and given him an eyeful. And what's more, he'd even called to make the date official. She would arrive at Saturday night's premiere of *The Little Orphan* on *his* lovely arm.

"Coming for lunch?" Ivan said some hours later as he stood in the doorway on his way out for lunch. The rest of the men had already left, eager to do their bit in the standoff and keep an eye on the evil Communists ruining their great country.

"Think I'll stay put."

"I'm not against them either you know," he nodded conspiratorially and left.

She wasn't a coward. She would drive through the front, not the delivery gate. Just as she'd done yesterday and the day before and the day before that. By now, two weeks in, the strike had grown to a great number, including at least half the women from Paint and Ink.

The best course of action was to drive through as quickly as possible, Maggie reasoned, so as not to interrupt their impassioned chanting. And whether she liked it or not, the slogans had begun to burn themselves into her brain. "Credit where credit's due—credit where credit's due—credit where credit's due," she muttered as she turned into Harley Drive.

But there was only a single voice as she approached the throng. Maggie pulled over, shutting off the engine lest the Pussycat give her away. "It's blackmail is what it is!" Milton's body shook as he thundered at the defectors through a loud-speaker. "Nothing but blackmail by a bunch of no-good layabouts and traitors," he leveled a murderous look at the very worst of them, Art, "every last one of you…"

"Save your war-talk for the real thing," a man screamed from the back of the pack. It was Walter, his arm slung about his wife's shoulder.

"Fair day's pay for a fair day's work!" Harriet yelled out, taking the lead in another heart-felt round.

"Put a sock in it!" Dora screamed as Milton rose on his toes, his fury brimming.

"You wanna keep your job?" he threatened as he stormed off, "then get the *hell* back to work!"

Maggie had seen enough. Her heart beat furiously and she swallowed hard…there was nothing to be ashamed of if she went round back. Besides, she planned on swinging by Morley Hall on her way home, a chore she'd been meaning to do so for some time now, lend a hand with the placards or supplies or something.

She turned the wheel, accelerating slowly to escape unnoticed, but when she glanced in the rearview mirror her heart sank. Harriet, Art, Walter and Dora had all witnessed her cowardly retreat.

"You okay?" Ivan asked later that afternoon as he unpacked a box of reference books, illustrated volumes on armory, submarines and aircraft. Only black-and-white—but as Ivan rightly pointed out, if Moogle McDoogle ended up piloting a purple or pink aircraft it would be all the same to him—so long as he had his pipe at the ready and a steady supply of pinto-beans. "Sure you're okay Maggie? You look a little peaky."

"Headache. I could do with some water."

"Coming right up," he made a swift about-turn and came back with a full glass.

"Thank you."

"You come through the back? Milt's out there giving 'em an earful."

"She sure did," Jack interjected. Maggie, fuming, retreated to her imagination, hammering Jack's body further into the dirt. He just couldn't help himself it seemed. "Yep, with her tail between her legs," he went on, whimpering like a dog to make his point clear.

"Hey let her be will you?" Ivan slammed down a book to get Jack's attention.

"Alright already—no need to snap your cap. Geez, can't a guy have a bit of fun?"

"Sure," Maggie rounded on him, "a guy *can*. And a guy *does*. But would a guy kindly mind if it's not at my expense for once?" That had done it, Maggie thought with satisfaction. Jack had finally seen fit to extract his extremely sticky nose from her business.

"I'm here," Maggie sang out that evening as she presented herself at the door of Morley Hall, "my—it's awful quiet in here." She peered over Dora's shoulder into union headquarters, the old church that had opened its doors to the organizers. There wan't much to see really, just a few people sitting around fold-out tables sedately, "I expected to see all guns blazing."

"Oh yeah? Sorry to disappoint." Dora held the door ajar without a hint she might be about to welcome the visitor in, "hold up a minute," she called over her shoulder to a man struggling with a box overflowing with tin mugs, "take them out back—Bert came through with a van…at last."

"Better late than never," the man said. He nodded at Maggie and took the mugs out.

"What do you want?" Dora asked gruffly.

"Well," Maggie said, patiently abiding Dora's stonewalling, "can I come in? You see I've a ton of ideas for fund-raising and the like—if the strike drags on that is."

"Oh it will if Milt don't come to the party."

"Here—" Maggie opened her purse and took out a ten-dollar bill. Dora, clearly unmoved by the generous donation, rejected it outright. "I thought we could start a fund for girls especially, then you can get your cough medicine and anything else you might want."

"Yeah?" Dora scoffed, "how bout a vacation in Havana?" Maggie, her head bowed, fiddled with her purse.

"But they had a fund at Dolman's didn't they?"

"That's right. And we already got one."

"Oh but you'll take it. Please." Maggie pressed the note into Dora's hand.

"Keep your money."

"Don't be stupid—"

"Listen—we don't want charity, we want folks willing to stick their necks out, folks who ain't afraid of getting 'em chopped off if it comes to that."

As the sound of footsteps came towards them Maggie stuffed the bill back in her purse. "Hey, what's going on?" Harriet said, wedging herself between them.

"See? I'm here, 1182 Juno Street," Maggie chirped, doing her best to ignore Dora, "at your service."

"So I see," Harriet frowned as she took in Maggie's brand-new Louis-heel T-straps, "say, nice shoes you got there. Lemmie guess, for the premiere right?"

"Thought I'd wear them in, nothing worse than blisters."

"Oh no," Dora rolled her eyes and snorted in disgust, "nothing worse than blisters."

"Why, I…" Maggie faltered. She straightened her spine and sniffed, "I see I'm not wanted round here…"

"Uh-huh, guess we'll see you later on," Dora said, glancing at Harriet, "we're sure looking forward to the premiere."

Chapter Twenty-Three

"Watch out," Ted said as Maggie side-stepped a patch of glass filaments, the aftermath of a dozen or so spent flashbulbs.

"Good heavens, so this is what it's like being a Hollywood sweetheart."

"Now you know why I avoid the limelight," Ted grinned, "too darned dangerous."

As he took her arm and escorted her into the Palace Theatre on Broadway, she glanced shyly at his face, the face she'd once considered a little handsome but now thought an awful lot more so. And even though she wouldn't have minded, there was no jangling of pockets tonight. Maybe he'd had the foresight to clear out the metal for the occasion...or perhaps her presence had a settling effect on him. Her heart glowed at the thought that it might.

Thankfully, inside the foyer the exploding flashes ceased. They'd arrived relatively early, or early enough. "Before all the crazy," he'd explained on the phone before showing up at her apartment rather *too* early. Caught by surprise, she'd dispensed with her ambitious plan to set her hair in a copy of Clara's solid waves—or as close as she could manage with her limited knowledge of things coiffure.

"I love my flower, it's adorable," Maggie said, feeling for the little yellow token she'd pinned to her hat, "what sort is it?"

"Some kind of daisy I guess." He'd plucked the bloom from the rockery at the top of the driveway, a patch of yellow that had only just caught his eye after three years of living at Mountfield Gates. "Strange I never noticed before," he mused, eyeing the minimalist bouquet.

"Lovely."

"Sure suits you," he cleared his throat, blinking and turning this way and that. Maggie, glowing from the compliment, watched as the parade of glamorous guests passed by.

"Champagne?" Maggie took two from the bar and sighed contentedly, "you know I think I might be lost for words...no that's not true is it? I'm *still* talking."

"Go right ahead."

"This is the most thrilling, wonderful night of my life," she beamed.

"To thrilling nights," Ted said, touching his glass to hers.

"To thrilling nights and lives, and to seeing the Orphan at long last...*and* my squirrel...Milton hasn't said anything about a meeting has he?"

"Nope. But you'll see her," he spun the glass-stem in his fingers and gazed over her shoulder.

"I guess so...one of these days," Maggie sighed, vowing to keep her frustrations at bay, put broken promises, ungrateful friends and horrible smug men to the back of her mind where they belonged for the time being. Tonight she would celebrate beating Independent to it, the hard work she and all her colleagues had sunk into the history-making film. "Here's to the Orphan—may she be Harley's biggest star yet," she raised her glass with a flirtatious smile, "and may her prince arrive sooner rather than later."

They ascended to their balcony seats and she peered behind her then down at the crowd below. "Where's Milt? Fashionably late I suppose."

"Something like that."

"I prefer early birds," Maggie said, lifting her champagne hastily and misjudging the distance between glass and face. She dried her nose with a quick swipe and peeked at Ted, hoping he hadn't noticed her little faux pas…if he had he wasn't making a song and dance about it like Art would've—teased her mercilessly for the pure hell of it.

She reached over, squeezed Ted's arm, and *The Little Orphan* began.

"Ask me that's forty-thousand dollars well spent," Maggie whispered as the fancy camera proved its worth with yet another spectacular rendition of fairy-tale turrets and snow-capped mountains.

"Twenty-eight thousand five hundred and ninety-five," Ted reminded her, leaning into her side.

"Beg your pardon—my mistake," Maggie said, grinning in the dark, "splendid," she murmured as the Orphan awaited her fate at the foot of the looming castle…

She kept her fingers and toes crossed, praying Ted would make a move and sling his arm about her shoulder and pull her close, but so far the night had remained strictly and disappointingly platonic. "Oh my…" Maggie muttered as the Orphan's locks swirled in the violent wind, "how we hated that scene." She frowned, recalling the pains the Paint and Inkers had taken to perfect the billowing tresses, "of course they're glorious but we damned near went blind in the doing, and I'm not kidding, Dora especially—"

"Keep it down will ya?" Clara hissed, swiveling in her seat to admonish her ex-colleague.

"Beg your pardon," Maggie whispered as Clara resumed her tentative snuggling, her head resting somewhat awkwardly on Milt's broad shoulder.

"The prince will come soon," Maggie said, her lips only a few inches from Ted's ear. She waited, hoping he might take the hint, and a moment later she was rewarded with the warm brush of skin as his hand searched for hers. She opened her palm and their hands closed together in a comfortable, loose cup—

"Shoot—" Maggie lunged forward instinctively but it was too late. The carton of popcorn tipped, emptying its contents onto the carpet in an eruption of weightless rocks, and as Ted bent to clean up the mess, their heads knocked together painfully at knee-level. She sat up, shifting her foot awkwardly to allow him room to scoop.

At last he emerged, harried and unsure of his next move, wondering—as indeed was she—if eating sullied popcorn were quite the right thing to do. "Here," Maggie said, taking charge of the situation. She placed the carton under the seat, dusted her hands then folded them in her lap, spying Ted from the corner of her eye…but his hand was nowhere near crossing the armrest border dividing their kingdoms.

And then it was all over. The Orphan and her prince finally united and done with waltzing on the frozen lake. The audience erupted in hoots, whistles and deafening applause, a sustained congratulation that seemed to go on forever. Maggie, searching for familiar names in the rolling credits, frowned.

It seemed Milton hadn't seen fit to name *any* of her colleagues for their hours of toil. Not a single one of his girls had been acknowledged, and nor had Art…and no mention of Ivan either. Evidently the only members of the Harley family deserving credit were John, Jack, the director, the producer, and their undisputed king and leader, Mr Milton *goddamned* Harley…

"Enough!" he hollered, standing to silence his admirers. But the applause only got louder, the theatre bursting into ear-splitting whistling and wild cheering. At last the noise subsided and the proud boss was finally permitted to leave the theatre with Clara in tow.

"Let's wait," Ted said, "till the crowd thins out."

"Yes all right."

Maggie, distracted, her anger mounting, stared at the screen. The audience had sure made their appreciation known—but Milton sure as hell didn't appreciate the women who'd busted their guts to make capital-H-history. She chewed her cheek, her mind grinding fast…no, the women's work was merely 'window-dressing', as Jack liked to called it. She snorted her contempt, her body stiff with anger. "Not one credit for us girls," she hissed loudly, suddenly aware of Ted's worried gaze, "why should only a few get all the glory? What about the rest of us…?"

"Not now." Ted stood, rattled by her change of mood. Her heart thumped and he turned, evidently keen to make his way out, crowd or no crowd.

"And what about Art?" Maggie rose to her feet, determined to make her feelings known, "the ogre was terrific. *He* got most of the laughs—boy Milt's sure got a nerve," she glared at Ted's back, daring him to respond, but to no avail.

Her stomach turned, her legs weak from adrenaline. She sunk back to her seat, swallowing and blinking fast. Ted hadn't even glanced back, not once, hadn't waited like a gentleman ought—as a matter of fact it looked as if he hadn't thought twice about it. She jumped to her feet and hurried after him, elbowing past patrons and pushing her way through to the crowded foyer below.

The familiar sound of chanting became louder. She turned to her colleagues gathered outside the glass doors, and, tossing her cloak over her shoulders, rushed out into the hullabaloo.

Chapter Twenty-Four

"Credit where credit's due—credit where credit's due!" The police had been called, were linked in a human chain to prevent strikers getting too close to the fur-clad ladies and well-to-do men awaiting their chauffeur-driven cars.

Art thrust his placard in the air, the Ogre with the warty face. "Get him with the sign will you?" a reporter said, motioning to his photographer as Milton's ex-employee posed for the shot, "how about you cosy up a little?"

"Sure."

As Art complied with the request Maggie joined the throng, Ted's words echoing in her ears. *Not now. Not now.* It was inevitable she supposed that he'd brush her off, dismiss her concerns with no care whatever—he was, when it came down to it, cut from the same stiff cloth as his brother…

"You bet," Art said to the microphone in his face, "the Harley family is a big fat lie and I tell you why. No family oughta treat it's members like Milton Harley does—we want a pay rise and full credits on all feature films, you got that?"

"And no more quotas—" Maggie burst in, thrusting herself into the circle and all at once feeling exhilarated, lifted up by a powerful, heady rush, "you get that?" She turned to the reporter but he'd moved on, distracted by Milton's arrival, flanked by minders and the ever-present Clara.

"There he goes!" Dora shouted, "the devil!" Milton turned to the congregation, his face red and nostrils streaming smoke as he jabbed a finger at Art.

"You, you're a *disgrace*, a *real* piece of work," he spat.

"Is that so?" Art growled, "well if I'm a disgrace then I guess that makes you a plain ole thief. Right?"

"Maggie? You coming?" Ted's arms hung by his side, his face tight.

"Not now," she raised her chin, defiant and determined to serve him a dose of his own medicine.

"Let's go," Ted said, insistent.

"Harriet—" Maggie waved, ignoring the curt invitation and feeling a surge of anger on behalf of her friend. Harriet sure as hell wouldn't be celebrating the Orphan's success tonight, drinking champagne in brand-new Louis-heel T-straps—she'd go home to a musky rooming-house with holey walls and an empty cookie-tin.

Maggie grabbed the reporter's arm. "Here's a scoop for you —some of us Harley girls can't afford to eat, how do you like that?" He shook her off, distracted by a scuffle taking place between a striker and a police officer. She turned to Ted, blinking rapidly, her emotions unrestrained, "what about Walter? He hasn't a whit of hope since you fired him—let alone pride," she indicated Milton with a nod, "and you oughta stand up to him for once."

Ted's face drained of color, "good night Maggie." He thrust his hands in his pockets, turned on his heel and disappeared into the crowd.

The chanting resumed with even greater vigor and Maggie, vowing to wipe Ted thoroughly from her mind, rushed to Harriet's side and relieved her of the heavy placard. "Give me that." She raised the sign and swayed it in the air, banishing Ted with the force of righteous cause, "more dollars now—throw away the quotas, more dollars now—throw away the quotas!"

"Communists!" Milton railed as a photographer dodged flailing arms to capture the studio boss mid-shout. Milton, his body suddenly convulsing in a violent fit, covered his mouth as he turned to leave.

"Not so fast—" Maggie sidestepped, blocking his way.

"What the hell do you want?" he spluttered.

"My cartoon—where is she? Where's my Lilly?" She held her ground, prepared to cop a blast.

"Now you listen up and you listen good—"

"Very well, I'm listening."

"Every damned yard of that film belongs to me you hear?"

"That's bunk!"

"It's a goddamned rule is what it is," he faced the cordoned-off strikers, "don't any of you dimwits read your contracts?"

"She's not yours at all," Maggie said, squaring up to the ranting Milton, her hands planted on her hips, "Lilly belongs to me and *he*—" she pointed at Art, "*he* created the ogre and just about every other critter that's made you a rich man. We want our fair share, a fair taking." She straightened, eyeing him as though they might swing pistols at any minute.

A storm of flashbulbs exploded, illuminating their stand-off as a crowd gathered round, onlookers hungry for spectacle, men in double-breasted suits, women in shimmering gowns and a gaggle of photographers vying to get a shot of Milton high on rage—not to mention the brave woman giving the big cheese a thorough shake-down.

"Think you can get away with anything don't you?" he hissed, poking at Maggie's face.

"Get away with what might I ask?" Maggie growled, "I don't see what I've gotten away with at all—except working my fingers to the bone to make your Orphan a success."

"You know what I'm getting at, your little night escapades

behind my back, sweet-talking Ed to get your way. Think you really had it made, huh? And to think I let it slip—boy was I wrong." Maggie's face burned as she heard Ted's voice behind her.

"Out of the way," he said, pushing his way back through to them, "Maggie, quit it—come with me."

"I won't quit at all. And I won't be rounded up," she said, furious to be treated like a dog in need of a master. He ought to stick up for her, stand up to his bully of a brother if he cared about her at all.

"Milt!" Ted rushed to his brother's side as another coughing fit struck. Milton buckled, his knees collapsing as the hacking overpowered his ability to stand.

"Baby!" Clara cried as she and his minders rushed to assist.

"Stand back—" Milton croaked, managing to shake them off and stepping back into hostile territory.

"Come on baby, forget it, come on home to momma—"

"Outta the way!" he cried, shucking off Clara's attempt to drag him into the waiting limousine. He shot Maggie an ominous smile. "You…you're fired," he said, strangely calm. Her jaw dropped as Milton turned to the rest of the traitors and delivered the bad news, "you're *all* fired—every last one of you."

Chapter Twenty-Five

*A*rt and Adelita pushed through the doors of Morley Hall and Maggie wondered at the strangeness of feelings. It was odd, no trace remained of the jumpy thrill she'd once felt in Art's presence. She smiled wistfully. Whatever fond feelings she'd had for the man had completely evaporated, like the tiniest puff of cloud in the widest, blue sky.

"Here she is, the turn-coat," Art drawled as they came towards her.

"Uh-huh. Ready to get to it," Maggie said, rubbing her hands. She'd arrived just before six that morning, and after a good deal of tossing and turning in the night, was eager to throw herself into the cause, shake free of rumination.

"Least they got him right this time," Art tossed the newspaper on the table. It seemed everyone had their own copy, Maggie, Harriet, Dora. The unflattering photo of Milton's tantrum was the talk of the town, and there was hope it might go a ways to turning the tide in the rebels' favor.

"The Fortune and the Fury," Maggie read out, "and look here —there's my foot," she said, pointing out the elegant shoe in the corner of the shot.

"Very photogenic," Art grinned and turned to Adelita. Now a

few days off were permitted at Dolmans she'd called in sick to join the action. "You remember Maggie?" He seemed wary, as though the two women might strap on spurs and fight like cockerels. She tutted at her man then regarded Maggie with admiration.

"I hear what you do. You brave."

"Why thank you."

"You give him what for."

"And I'm very glad of it."

As Maggie announced her intention to find Harriet she swallowed away sadness. In the blink of an eye her life had flipped on end. She'd lost her job, ownership of her cartoon, and the keenest of all her losses—her budding romance with Ted.

Their night had begun so wonderfully and soured so, so terribly. But she supposed there was nothing to be done about it now. And there was certainly nothing left to lose. They'd all been tossed aside like junk and Uncle Milt deserved everything he got —and more…even if he *was* ill. She felt a sudden flutter of worry and shooed it away, while coals burned in her gut she would put them to good use.

"Our hero," Harriet cried, opening her arms to greet her friend, "glad you could make it comrade."

"You and me both."

"Finally…" Harriet rolled her eyes and laughed.

"Uh-huh. Pinned my colors to the mast."

"With the newspapers onside and your foot there'll be no stopping us. So—ready to get to it?"

"Sure am," Maggie said as she spotted Walter fixing a placard with a wind or two of tape, "how is he?"

"On the wagon five days and counting…but we'll see." Harriet prized open a tin of paint and passed Maggie a tattered brush.

"Seen better days," Maggie said of the hardened, ratty tip.

"Hey beggars can't be choosers okay?"

"No. But they can wash their brushes."

"Fair point sergeant. So…how was she, our Orphan?"

"Marvelous," Maggie said, emitting a dreamy sigh, "the most wonderful film in the world."

"That's what they said in the papers," Harriet admitted grudgingly.

As Maggie stirred the gooey paint with her sub-optimal tool she recalled her favorite scene of all, the two hands clasped together in the darkness, the brief romantic interlude that had turned all too quickly to slapstick. She wiped off excess paint and began her lettering, determined to forget all that. "And the Prince came to her rescue?" Harriet asked meaningfully.

"Oh yes," Maggie said, quashing the bud of sorrow that would surely bloom if she wasn't careful…Ted *hadn't* come to her rescue, he'd made his choice and she'd made hers. There was nothing more to be done about it, they belonged on different sides of the fence and that was one big fact.

An hour later later they piled into cars and drove to the picket-line, the mood becoming jubilant as they approached the frontline. "Look—" Harriet shouted, pointing to the huge gathering waiting for the action to begin. She stood up, waved, and jumped out of the Pussycat. "See? What I tell you? He ain't got a hope in hell now."

"How many? Four hundred?" Art guessed. He let out a rousing whistle and chanting broke out, a human chorus of unity and strength.

"Is loud," Adelita said.

"Boy you must get a real kick out of striking," Maggie laughed as they unpacked stuffed car trunks.

"I love this man," Adelita said simply.

"Aw, shucks," Art mugged. He wandered off, leaving the ladies to take care of details.

Over the past weeks the setup had become rather elaborate. On top of fold-out chairs, tables and basic supplies—coffee, crackers and tinned goods, there were books, magazines, comics, cushions, sun-hats, a couple of large umbrellas and a much coveted footstool.

"Keep a hold of that," Harriet advised as Maggie extracted the unusual accessory, "rule is, whoever gets it plays boss."

"Listen up," Art said, addressing the gathering with the aid of a loud-speaker, "until you get proper notice you're all still Harley employees." The crowd burst into cheering, then booed like cows lowing in a field. "Milt's nothing but a bully—the worst kind of bully." The booing intensified, an almost musical effect Maggie decided...if one tuned in the right way—in fact it was a bit like jazz. She inhaled sharply, determined to forget.

"Bad news," Harriet said as she scanned a sheet of paper secured to the fence.

"What is it?" Dora asked.

"What a piece of work," Harriet scoffed, "seems like Milt took the time to write it himself. Figures."

As Harriet read out the handwritten list of official firings, Maggie, despite her resolve to remain staunchly anti-Harley, felt a wave of relief. It at least proved Milton was still kicking, she hadn't killed him off with her very public humiliation...and the Orphan's success would surely go a ways to offset his distress—not that he deserved any sympathy from her or anyone else for that matter. She clamped her cheek, unable to forget his body-rattling cough.

"That coffee done yet?" Art called out. Maggie shook her head, mumbling as she lit the gas-cooker on loan from Harriet and Walter's cramped room. It didn't seem to matter what side of the fence she was on, her role as coffee-maker had remained unchanged.

"Not yet—but you'll let us know when it is won't you?" She linked arms with Adelita and led her away, "some of us oughta go round back," Maggie suggested as they met up with Harriet, Dora and Walter, "block off the delivery gate."

"We got it covered," Harriet informed her as she heaved a bundle of placards on end and doled them out to the empty-handed, "got a tipoff from a friend of yours, over there," she nodded at Ivan, helping Walter hoist the group's pride and joy—the largest of the banners at almost thirty feet and depicting Milton with his customary horns and forked-tongue.

"Take it out to the main street," Harriet instructed.

"Harriet—" Maggie began in a worried tone. She pointed to the motorcar approaching at an alarming speed.

"Relax, it's just Milt," Harriet said, evidently unruffled.

"Hey! Slow down!" Maggie yelled, her eyes wide with fear. After all, there was no telling what a desperate man might do—a man with a grand ego would surely strike back with avengeance.

"Does it every time," Harriet said as the Rolls-Royce slowed to walking pace without sending anyone flying like bowling-pins. "You don't scare us *Mr.*" Harriet hoisted her placard and the chanting began, strikers surrounding Milt's car and blocking it's passage with human-powered resistance.

"Fair day's pay for a fair day's work—fair day's pay for a fair day's work!" Maggie shouted at the top of her lungs. She'd managed to get to the front, close enough to peer in the window, past the figure leaning out of sight to Milton, his face set in a gritted clench.

"Thief! Thief! Thief! Thief!" Fists beat on car windows and Maggie, consumed with anxiety, dropped back. At last the car escaped, speeding away to safety behind the great iron gates.

"Bastard's running scared," Walter cursed as Maggie felt her heart constrict. Milt had seemed so diminished, shrunken, as if physically withered by the ordeal…what if he *was* terribly ill?

"Poor thing," Maggie said without thinking. She caught Art's exasperated look.

"Oh no you don't," he said, waving a warning finger, "can't have it both ways."

"I know, but he's sick—not well."

"You got that right. Sick in the head."

The days passed calmly enough and Maggie found herself sufficiently distracted with talk. Animation, politics, movies—or just
plain kidding around. Unfortunately her own store of jokes had
dried up on day one but Harriet's supply was positively unending.
And only a small part of the day was spent chanting or booing
like cows. And then there were the passers-by beeping in support,
or the occasional sticky-beak coming close enough to satisfy
curiosity but staying far enough away to signal ambivalence.

She might have been content if it weren't for the strong desire
to burst through the gates and demand the immediate return of
her cartoon. Run as far away from the whole mess as she possibly
could, board the next train back east to the comfort of her Park
Slope home, forget all about the ache in her heart that just
wouldn't let up. And then there were the disturbing rumors.
Rumors regarding Harley's finances that were fast gaining
weight…Maggie, her mind churning, felt another cold wave of
fear.

Dissatisfied with the half-cocked caricature of Art and his
megaphone, she put aside her sketchbook and plucked a magazine from the pile, flipping it open to a random page. Country
houses in upstate New York…how to find the kind of furnishings
that showed the whole world you 'just knew'.

She felt a sharp pang as she recalled Ted's music room, the
sanctuary away from his troubles. If she'd complied with his
wishes and gone with him the night of the premiere she might
well be an expert at Chopsticks by now, not wasting time sitting
about reading silly magazines with a heart that felt as heavy as
lead.

She scowled, returning to the particulars of the Boston home-
maker's pelmet dilemma and humming a tune she hadn't been
able to shake since Ted had blown it into her brain via a shiny,

brass tube. She wondered if he'd had the time or inclination to practice lately…she very much doubted it…perhaps she ought to just telephone instead of driving herself crazy with fruitless speculation. After all, the card with his number was still in the little box right by her bed—

"*Uptown Downtown*," Walter said, breaking into her thoughts.

"I beg your pardon?" Maggie closed the magazine and squinted up at him.

"The tune."

"Huh?"

"The tune, you're humming a tune." Walter took one of the newspapers and tossed aside a copy of *The Hollywood Reporter* in the process—they were the enemy—Milton's buddies through and through, "*Uptown Downtown* by Chuck Johnson," he explained.

"Why yes…Chuck," Maggie said, suddenly recalling the leg aficionado who'd materialized in the giant sofa-chair, "matter of fact we're acquainted."

"You're kidding?"

"Nope, we had the great fortune of meeting quite recently. A terrific party, just terrific."

"You don't say?" Walter regarded her with unfettered envy, "can you swing me an invite next time? Boy, what I'd give to meet Chuck Johnson…"

"I don't suppose that'll happen," she said, regret in her voice.

"Plan on keeping him to yourself huh?"

"It's only…" she paused, unsure if she ought go on, if the mention of a certain someone might set off Walter's ire, "he's a friend of Ted's." She held her breath, preparing to hear the worst about the man she liked best, how he'd been the cause of great personal misery and cruel enough to kick a man when he was down—metaphorically speaking of course—Ted was far too gentle to strike another man standing or otherwise, not in a million years.

"Hows about an autograph then?" Walter said, surprisingly calm at the mention of Ted, "think you can swing that?"

"I'll see what I can do." Maggie smiled, pleased for Harriet's sake, sobriety seemed to be doing Walter a world of good. She stretched her arms lazily and let out a contrived yawn, "if I'd known striking was so relaxing I'd have come earlier," she joked. Just then Art rushed by.

"Gather round, there's word from inside," he called out, upending an empty fruit-crate and mounting the makeshift podium. "Listen up," he hollered. The crowd hushed, hoping and praying for good news, "looks as if Milt's coming round to our way of thinking." Cheers rang out and Maggie scrambled to her feet, her heart in her mouth as Art shushed the crowd again. "I'll be jumping ship to Independent when this is all over, no offense… but looks as if *you* lot just got your jobs back—" The air exploded in gleeful whoops for a good minute or so then calmed to excited chatter. Art shrugged casually and grinned, "all we gotta do now is get you more dough."

A collective sigh of disappointment ensued. "No pay rise? Where is that cheap bastard?" Harriet scowled and shook her fist, "too chicken to show his ugly mug I bet—why I'll give him a piece of my mind." She thrust her placard high and burst into another round of impassioned chanting, "fair day's pay for a fair day's work—fair day's pay for a fair day's work!"

Chapter Twenty-Six

"Uh-huh, I will," Maggie assured her father later that evening, "just as soon as we get what we want." Then, when the strike was over and Milton had blown off all the steam boiling inside his cauldron-like being, she would make it her business to get Squirrel Lilly back. "Even if it kills me," she declared, "I don't care what he says about fine-print—that cartoon is mine."

Her father agreed, Milton was too stubborn for his own good, too inclined to pin labels on those with the courage to disagree, a most unpleasant fellow indeed. "Well yes…I suppose he is," Maggie said, suddenly retreating from her own recently-aired opinion.

Perhaps it was time to get a lawyer. Her father knew a good one who'd made the move to California for health's sake. Particularly experienced in patents, matters of ownership and the like, as it happened. "No—no lawyers Paps, I'll figure it out," Maggie said, shuddering at the thought of Ted receiving a letter served on her behalf.

Milton hadn't been seen for over a week. Newspapers speculated with stories running the gamut. He was gravely ill in hospital. He'd been seen meeting privately with an executive from

Independent. He was enjoying a cowardly getaway in Florida. "And I'll post the picture tomorrow," Maggie promised, fingering the clipping of her famous foot, "rather a hoot really…and I've made some terrific pals—all thanks to the Wagner Act."

Her father chuckled and she felt the pull of home…the house that had been a haven for most of her life, the leaves that would soon fall in Central Park, the magnificent blazing of orange, yellow and red. "Oh I do miss it," she said, keenly aware of the simple remedy her father had already recommended, a lengthy and most imminent visit.

The next day Maggie cast her eye over the familiar gathering, Harriet and Walter bickering over something said or unsaid, Art distributing himself between strikers to spread the latest intelligence. The news was official. All jobs were guaranteed in exchange for ending the strike. But the vote was unanimous. They hadn't come this far only to give up at the last hurdle. "It's insulting is what it is," Harriet said, passing round the document sent down by one of Milton's heavies, his eyes hidden under a lowered hat.

"Why he rips our livelihoods away then offers them back as if it were the most generous gift in the world," Maggie said, utterly frustrated with the impasse. If it went on much longer she was sure to lose the last of her fast-dwindling spirits. Every morning she arrived at the gates hoping the strike would end and they could all get back to work. Of course she was free to cross the picket-line and take-up tools any time she liked—and a few of the strikers had done just that—scabs who'd abandoned the cause at the eleventh hour. As far as Maggie was concerned, that line of action was out of the question…unthinkable.

However, she figured, there were other options. Now with her greater knowledge and experience she might set up her own fledgeling company back home in New York, just as Milton had started out, renting space in a small, cramped office. There was no reason why she oughtn't do the same, after all, she'd already discussed the matter with her father and secured his backing, financial and otherwise. "Why not?" Maggie muttered to herself as she stole the royal footstool from under Harriet's nose.

"Hey!"

"Nope. I'm boss. Fetch me a gin sling—on the double you hear?"

Half an hour later, sufficiently informed as to eyebrow styles and making the most of a humble potato, Maggie tossed the well-thumbed magazine aside. Useful information she supposed, if she were ever required to peel a potato, if, for example, she were ever to marry…but then Ted would likely do a far better job of it than she ever could—if his orange-peel trick was anything to go by…

Her throat constricted and she fought back tears. The way things were she might never discover if Ted knew his way around a potato or not, let alone his true feelings with regard to the strike…or her for that matter. Did he *truly* side with his brother? Maggie wondered as she turned to the puzzles on page forty-three…or was he just another victim of Milt's infamous boot?

Cars came and went but the crossword, lying in Maggie's lap, remained unsolved. After more than half an hour of filling in boxes and rubbing out letters, the only cracked clue was the ubiquitous three-lettered, flightless Australian bird. She glanced at the road, yet again hoping the taller Harley brother would make a show.

She'd asked around, casually, but like Milt, Ted hadn't been seen coming or going via foot, automobile, bicycle, air-ship or magic-carpet in the past week. In fact she'd begun to suspect the worst—Milton's illness *was* as serious as some of the newspapers had begun to report.

"For goodness sake he's not a gangster," Maggie exclaimed, breaking into a tense conversation between Art and Bert.

According to Bert, armed police might arrive at any minute to break up their little party.

"Depends how you define gangster," Bert said, convinced of Milton's deeply nefarious character. The studio boss was quite the type to pack a few thousand dollars in a suitcase if it meant the right kind of return.

"The man isn't well," Maggie said, greatly irritated. She glared at five-across, the Asian spice determined to stump her progress. After a few more attempts she threw the thing aside and resumed her self-appointed role of detective, looking out for rats in the ranks, strikebreakers and phonies masquerading as men and women of good conscience. So far none had been found out, but she had her suspicions about one particular fellow. "Over there," she said, pointing to a young man in the distance.

"That's Bert's kid," Art raised a brow and grinned.

"Well tell him to quit snooping about."

"I'll let him know," Art said, leaving Maggie to her speculations. She closed her eyes and tried to clear her mind, but once again Ted rushed back and she felt the familiar sickness in her heart.

"Hey, look sharp Mags." Maggie's eyes flew open at the sound of Harriet's voice. "Here comes trouble," Harriet nodded at the road, the car turning into Harley drive…the maroon car with the immaculate paintwork and adorable driver, "your prince…better late than never."

Maggie's heart missed a beat as she scrambled to her feet and stood stiffly. "You're not going soft are you?" Harriet said with a warning look.

"Soft?" Maggie flushed, indignant, "I'm as solid as a rock. Give me that—" She yanked the sign from Harriet's hands, her breath caught in her throat as she turned to Ted's car, steadily approaching at a sober pace.

Had he seen her yet…? Her cheeks burned and her knees felt weak. She took a step back, her grip loosening on the wooden paling, the desire to wield the placard suddenly swamped by a stronger one to toss the thing aside.

"Well?" Harriet raised her brows, "you gonna wave that thing around or take it home and roast it?" Maggie hung back as Harriet rushed forward to fortify the troops.

"Let him have it!" Art yelled out from behind the pack.

"Fair day's pay for a fair day's work—fair day's pay for a fair day's work!" The sun hit the windshield, momentarily obscuring Ted's face. His hands tightened on the wheel, his eyes trained to the front. Maggie, rooted to the spot with her heart sinking, chanted under her breath, her lips barely moving, "credit where credit's due—credit where credit's due…"

The car slowed, nosing through the crowd. Men mounted the running board and yelled through the windows, fists pummeling the roof as the vehicle inched through.

"Stop—!" Maggie lurched forward, desperate to reach the man now surrounded by enemies. There was a crash, the sound of shattering glass. "Ted!" She pushed through and rapped on the roof just as the car broke free and sped away. "Who the hell did that?" she demanded, furious, "is he hurt? Did anyone see—?" She fought back tears, her heart plunging to new depths as she saw Ted get out of his car and hurry away to safety.

"Come along," Harriet said, leading Maggie to a quiet spot away from the action.

She sat, stunned by the encounter. The whole thing had happened so quickly, and the thought Ted had been hurt struck her as truly horrific. "He'll be fine," Harriet said, rubbing Maggie's arm comfortingly, adamant no Harley blood had been spilled in the altercation, "just a bust window is all."

"That sure was a blast," Bert said, approaching them with a skip in his step, "what we got here? More oranges?" He scooped one from the crate.

"Found 'em right over there," Harriet pointed to a spot near the boundary wall, "same as the last lot." She took one herself and tossed another to Maggie, who, despite her state of discombobulation, caught the cheery fruit in sure hands. She stared, unseeing as her thumb sunk into the spongy flesh, the zingy smell rushing to her nose.

"They're from Ted," she muttered, staring at the suddenly wondrous fruit.

"What?" Harriet's brow furrowed.

"They're from Ted," Maggie repeated. She smiled, warm thoughts enveloping her being, her spirits rejuvenated.

"You sure about that?"

"Uh-huh." Maggie's heart expanded in a rush of gratitude… the oranges had to be from him—where else could they have come from? "The sweetest in the world," she gushed.

"Guess the guy can't be all bad," Harriet allowed.

"He's lovely," Maggie said, as much to herself as anybody else.

"Oh sure, a real swell," Bert scoffed. He dumped his orange and gave it a nasty kick, "keeping the peasants happy is he?" He scooped up the bruised ball and jettisoned it over the wall to make his feelings known.

"Hey!" Harriet exclaimed.

"For goodness sake stop!" Maggie bellowed.

But it was too late, a contingent of men fell upon the crate like a plague of locusts and began taking aim themselves, flinging the fruit at Harley Studios in a contest of ability and strength.

"How *dare* you!" Maggie growled, her anger boiling to rage as the disgraceful assault escalated to gleeful free-for-all.

"Kid's got an arm like a slingshot," Bert said proudly as his sneaky-looking son took aim at Wild Willie's statue, "bonus points for the head."

"Idiots," Harriet shook her head, disgusted.

"Now look here—" Maggie rounded on the kid, catching his arm as he took aim, "that's good fruit, the best fruit in the world and you're a fool to waste it."

"Leave off lady—" he shot her a look of pure contempt, snatched the orange back and tossed it over the wall. Maggie blanched, appalled by the ungrateful circus flying in the face of Ted's kindness.

"Home," Maggie muttered as another orange missed Willie's head by a hair. She felt a sharp stab of loneliness, a longing for her father and all that was familiar. She pressed her palms to her gut as Walter arrived on the scene at his wife's request.

"Okay pal—quit it," he said, turning Bert's kid away.

"He's back," Art called out as the final orange fell to the ground with an ugly splat. Maggie turned to see the tall figure behind the iron gate, his chin smudged with a mess of dried blood.

She rushed to the gates just as an envelope sliced through the bars and fell to the ground. "Ted," she cried softly, without hope of being heard. He'd completed his business. Was already in retreat, his hands in his pockets and back to the mob.

Art ripped open the envelope like a bear swiping salmon from a stream. He scanned the contents and waved the letter in the air to the sound of collective triumph. "We did it! We've won! He's backed down!"

Starting from the next day, all Harley employees would take up their posts with a pay rise and work no more than eight hours a day. "And no more quotas down at Paint and Ink—how bout that ladies?"

"What about credits?" someone called out. Art scanned the letter and looked up.

"Lead animators only. But there's a cherry on top I think you'll be pleased about. Uh-huh, *mighty* pleased as a matter of fact…" he paused teasingly then continued, "you no longer work for the devil, so to speak—"

"What?" Maggie frowned, confused by the sudden turn of events.

"Yep. Harley just got bought out. A nice little takeover."

"Independent?" Harriet guessed.

"You got it. Welcome aboard folks."

Maggie's head swirled. She felt too hot, too confined—in great need of space. She had to get away. To breath, to think…to sort her racing thoughts. She half-listened as Art revealed the details. The rumors were true. The Harley ship had been sinking for years, sinking into a hole so deep the only solution was a bail-out from their biggest competitor. Independent hadn't beaten them to it, but in the end Milton had been beaten… *The little Orphan* couldn't save him now.

"Hey—where you going?" Harriet followed as Maggie made her escape, tears brimming and chin wavering ominously. She stifled a sob, angry with herself. She ought to be glad, positively overjoyed, but all she felt was pain and turmoil, a terrible ripping in her heart. And Ted *had* seen her at the gate. Of that she was certain—she'd seen the brief flicker of recognition in his eyes, the unmistakable look of hurt and betrayal.

She fought her way through the crowd. Tears would flow at any minute. She broke into a run, desperate to be alone and sure she would never see Ted again. Most likely he was packing up this very minute, making plans to get as far away from the place as possible, as far away from *her* as possible…

She wrenched open the Pussycat's door, and after much fumbling with the key, revved the engine in a loud roar. "Mags—where you going?" Harriet yelled, sprinting towards her as Maggie threw the stick into gear and stamped on the accelerator.

She sped away without looking back.

Chapter Twenty-Seven

*S*he barely remembered the drive home. Collapsed on her bed she stared at the pillow, now thoroughly wet from tears. Everything had changed yet everything remained the same. The little chair in need of a fresh coat of paint, the pile of unruly clothes clumped in the corner, the bright Mexican quilt from the noisy downtown market…

She rolled to her side with her eyes shut tight and wished it would rain. Or hail. Or snow—that she'd wake to find the streets enveloped in an icy, white carpet. Anything but the monotony of the sky she'd once claimed as a companion to her growing fortune. It's cheeriness irked her now, in fact she couldn't stand the damned sight of it.

The telephone rang on and on. It would be Harriet of course. But she didn't dare pick up. A friendly voice might set off more tears just when she'd tamed the flow. And what could she say? That she'd found herself well and truly lost in affairs of the heart? That she'd fallen for Ted Harley's quiet strength and kindness, that she couldn't for all her might shake the longing for him—the terrible sensation that felt every bit as sharp as it did dull.

The truth was, Maggie realized, her very being ached for Ted and his blood-smeared chin. *So,* she thought to herself, this was what *it* felt like…

"Maggie Goodwin, quit acting the fool." Her legs swung over the side of the bed and she sat up, determined to set her will against misery, against fruitless what-ifs and should-haves and never-wills.

She hiccuped, gulped, then padded to the bathroom to freshen up, to go on as she had before. After all, tomorrow would come, then another tomorrow, then another after that. And the gloom was bound to lift sooner or later, time healing wounds and all that. Besides, Maggie reasoned as she turned the faucet and bent over the wash-tub, perhaps Independent had different ideas about ownership, fine-print that was at least visible to the human eye for example.

She pressed the damp cloth to her eyes. Just as soon as she'd repaired the damage she'd set about her next move. Pack away the past and step into her future.

The telephone rang out again and she marched towards it bravely, letting out breath in a long, steady stream.

"Harriet, I thought it might be you."

"Too bad about the oranges, the kid's a creep."

"Yes…I rather think he is. Where are you? Celebrating the good news I expect?"

"Uh-huh, no champagne, but plenty of beer. You coming along?"

"Sure. Why not."

She arranged her face into its usual lovely state, powder applied and hair patted down. And with the addition of a splash of red across her lips, still a little plump from weeping, she looked every bit presentable and respectable. She smiled at her reflection and gave a little nod.

Despite the hollowed-out feeling inside there was still hope, a faint fluttering of wings, a butterfly or perhaps a bee—poised to take flight to the next open flower.

· · ·

With hat jammed over brown curls she pressed the pedal and picked up speed, but as the turnoff to Morley Hall came into sight she drove onwards, towards the hills and her very singular purpose…

Her grip slipped on the wheel, her hands clammy as the winding road climbed higher, her heart hammering in her chest as she arrived at Mountfield Gates. But there were no welcoming lights to greet her this time, no charming lanterns or toy-soldiers ready to comply with her every desire. The great, iron gates were unguarded, gaping…thrown wide-open.

A truck barreled out, blaring its horn and forcing her to stop. She crunched the gear-stick into reverse and lurched back in a panic, the hood of the Pussycat barely missing the large vehicle already rollicking down the treacherous road.

She looked around, fearing the worst. The place seemed so empty, abandoned, as though trees had been ripped out by the roots or some other vital element had gone missing. She took a moment to settle her nerves and turned her gaze to the front door.

The bell rang and fear rushed to her throat. She eyed the bush at the top of the drive, the bush with the pretty yellow flowers that suited her so well. Adrenaline coursed through her limbs and she prayed for composure. To somehow find the strength to do what her heart asked.

At last the door swung open. Her heart leapt.

"Yes? I help you, miss?" the maid said, regarding Maggie with irritation. She lowered a great sack and let it rest on the floor.

"Is Mr Harley available? Is he here…? Only I don't see his car…" Maggie craned her neck, scanning the yard.

"You think he leave in sun?" she shook her head, "he park in garage."

"Yes of course he does," Maggie said, her smile vanishing at the sight before her, the stacked boxes and general air of flux, the ominous smell of soap and Clorox. It was exactly as she feared. Ted was leaving. Packing his bags and shipping out. Not just Harley Studios but most likely California as well, just as she'd urged him to do—break free of his brother's yoke and find his own calling.

"Is he in?" Maggie repeated, her panic rising and cursing herself for waiting so long when she could have simply picked up the telephone.

"You wait, I find." The maid propped the bag against the wall and mounted the stair-case, leaving Maggie to her sweaty palms and desperate thoughts.

Soon there were footsteps and she blinked away fear, her heart in her mouth as Ted descended. "I take rubbish then come back," the maid said, glancing over her shoulder as she departed.

"Hallo," Maggie managed.

He balked, his face aflame at the sight of her. She bowed her head, unable to speak now she'd found herself alone with the man who'd stolen her heart, "I've been terribly worried…" She felt his searching gaze and returned it with her own, "is he…is Milton alright?"

"For now," Ted said, standing motionless before her.

"Where—what's all this?" her voice wavered, "you're leaving?"

"Tonight. Soon as we're done here." He walked past her out to the front porch, staring at the view he'd soon leave. Maggie, her nerves affray, followed him out on shaky legs.

"It's awful sudden isn't it? Up and leaving just like that—and the takeover, such a shock…"

"Milt took some convincing but it's for the best."

"The best, yes…"

"Been walking a fine line for years."

"Oh I see," Maggie managed, her breath quick and shallow, "but where will you go?" Her voice emerged in a strained squeak.

"Not far. Santa Monica as a matter of fact."

"Thank goodness for that," she blurted out, thoroughly relieved, "getting some sea air?" His frown softened.

"Uh-huh. Closer to work too."

"Oh?"

"Douglas Aircraft," he said, brightening at the prospect.

"All the nuts and bolts—yes, you'll enjoy that," she looked at her shoes, lost for words. "Ted I…"

"What is it Maggie? What do you want?"

She wanted to reach out and touch him, link her arm through his and squeeze—or better still, feel his firm, soft hand in hers. "It's awful. Wasting your lovely oranges like that when you've been so kind…" She heard the familiar jangle of metal in pocket.

"And?"

"Well. I wanted to thank you for everything you've done." She looked up, hoping his expression had warmed even more, but it seemed the thawing had come to an end…instead, a very dark look had taken over.

"Good ole Ted huh?" he said, his tone biting, "good ole Ted."

"Oh but you *are*," Maggie rushed on, "if it weren't for you I'd have never got Lilly up and running—"

"No?" he snorted bitterly, "I'd wager you'd find a way." He hung his head and Maggie, her hopes for reconciliation fading, stiffened. The reunion wasn't going as she'd hoped—in fact Ted had taken a step in a most unsavory direction, down a tired path for which she no longer had any patience.

"Now what do you mean by that?" her voice quavered dangerously.

"You know what I mean."

"No I'm afraid I don't."

"So you think me that dull do you?"

"Dull? I don't think anything of the sort." Maggie colored, half in anger and half in shame. She had thought him a little dull, but only in the beginning. She didn't think him dull now—only kind, gentle and strong. "I suppose I'm just another Clara am I? A gold digger—is that it?" Maggie said, ripping off the bandage and staring straight at the wound.

"Least she loves him—I'll give her that," he held Maggie's gaze, daring her to do the same.

"Yes," she looked away, flustered, "she does love him…very much."

"You want your film is that it?"

"What? Of course I want it—"

"I guessed as much."

He turned to go inside and she followed blindly, desperate to make her feelings known but not knowing how. And what was he talking about anyhow? Did *he* have her Lilly?

He took a package from a stack of boxes and tossed it into her arms. She looked down at the brown-paper package addressed to her apartment, ripped it open and held the precious reel in her hands.

"Faster than the postal service," he said with a snort. Tears welled in her eyes.

"You can't know what this means to me—"

"One last favor huh?" He walked away, seemingly finished and she followed, gathering her thoughts before she spoke, her voice firm and low.

"You don't have a single idea do you?" He stopped in his tracks and turned to face her.

"Go right ahead and tell me—what don't I know?"

"What it's like to be a woman, what it's like to be treated as second-class at every turn…don't you see? You offered help and I took it—why shouldn't I?" She gazed into his soulful eyes and felt a torrent of emotion course through her being, "and if I happen to have fallen for a very helpful fellow in the meantime then I can't help that either—" she broke off, shocked at how easily her confession had come in the end, "the truth of the matter is I care for you Ted…very much as it happens."

"You do?"

"Uh-huh."

His face flushed with surprise and delight and his eyes blazed with joy, "come—"

He took her hand and led her up the stairs, along the hallway and into one of the rooms. She looked around, frowning, confused.

"Sit," he said, dragging two chairs to the middle of the bare room, and, before she had time to think he drew the curtains and she plonked herself down. "Let me have that." The package slipped from her lap and she twisted round as Ted loaded the projector at the far end of the room. Her mouth dropped open.

"I planned on showing you after the premiere," he said as he threaded the film through the rollers, "but then you figured on getting yourself mixed up in a brawl."

"Squirrel Lilly and the Giant Turtle-Wave..." Maggie murmured, her eyes gleaming in the projected light as Lilly swung from a branch and landed in the stream with her boat. "Oh my!" she cried as the turtle-hump emerged from the deep and her intrepid squirrel set to surfing, balancing on the wave with the tip of her magnificent tail...

"And not *too* much arthritis," Maggie said, smiling through tears of joy.

"Nope," Ted agreed, "not too much."

And as the leaf-boat sailed into the sunset, he turned to the lady-animator and pressed his lips to hers, a soft, lingering union that was only just the beginning.